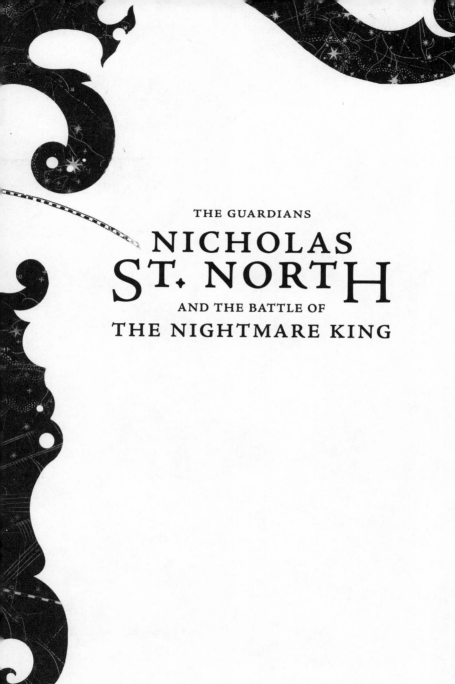

THE GUARDIANS

NICHOLAS
ST. NORTH

AND THE BATTLE OF

THE NIGHTMARE KING

Pitch, the Nightmare King

THE GUARDIANS

NICHOLAS
ST. NORTH

AND THE BATTLE OF

THE NIGHTMARE KING

by WILLIAM JOYCE &
LAURA GERINGER

◆

with illuminations by WILLIAM JOYCE

Atheneum Books for Young Readers
NEW YORK ◆ LONDON ◆ TORONTO ◆ SYDNEY ◆ NEW DELHI

Atheneum Books for Young Readers
An imprint of Simon & Schuster Children's Publishing Division
1230 Avenue of the Americas, New York, New York 10020
For information about special discounts for bulk purchases, please contact Simon & Schuster
Special Sales at 1-866-506-1949 or business@simonandschuster.com.
The Simon & Schuster Speakers Bureau can bring authors to your live event.
For more information or to book an event, contact the Simon & Schuster Speakers Bureau
at 1-866-248-3049 or visit our website at www.simonspeakers.com.
Book design by Lauren Rille
The text for this book is set in Adobe Jenson Pro.
The illustrations for this book are rendered in a combination of charcoal,
graphite, and digital media.
Manufactured in the United States of America
0811 FFG
First Edition
10 9 8 7 6 5 4 3 2 1
Library of Congress Cataloging-in-Publication Data
Joyce, William, 1957–
Nicholas St. North and the battle of the Nightmare King / by William Joyce and
Laura Geringer ; illumination by William Joyce. — 1st ed.
p. cm. — (The Guardians ; 1)
Summary: Nicholas St. North, a daredevil swordsman seeking treasure in the fiercely guarded
village of Santoff Claussen finds, instead, the great wizard Ombric Shalazar and a battle
against the Nightmare King and his evil Fearlings.
ISBN 978-1-4424-3048-8
ISBN 978-1-4424-3575-9 (eBook)
[1. Good and evil—Fiction. 2. Adventure and adventurers—Fiction.
3. Nightmares—Fiction. 4. Wizards—Fiction. 5. Heroes—Fiction. 6. Moon—
Fiction. 7. Santa Claus—Fiction.] I. Bass, L. G. (Laura Geringer). II. Title.
PZ7.J857Nic 2011
[Fic]—dc23 2011015074

———◆———

To
Jack Joyce,
A fine, upstanding young rascal,

And to his sister,
Mary Katherine,
Who was fierce, fun, and kind

——————◄ W. J. ►——————

Contents

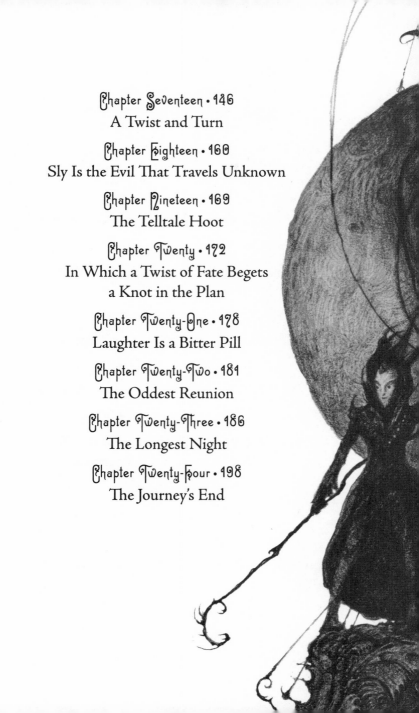

CHAPTER ONE

In Which the Great War Is Renewed

THE BATTLE OF THE Nightmare King began on a moonlit night long ago. In the quiet town of Tanglewood, a small boy and his smaller sister woke with a start. Like most children (and some adults at one time or another), they were afraid of the dark. They each slowly sat up in bed, clutching their covers around themselves like a shield. Too fearful to rise and light a candle, the boy pushed aside the curtains and peered out the window, looking for the only other light to be seen during these long-ago nights—the Moon. It was there, full and bright.

At that moment a young moonbeam shot down from the sky and through the window. Like all beams, it had a mission: *Protect the children.*

The moonbeam glowed its very hardest, which seemed to comfort the two. One, then the other, breathed a sleepy sigh and lay back down. In a few moments they were once again asleep. The moonbeam scanned the room. All was safe. There was nothing there but shadows. But the beam sensed something beyond the room, beyond the cabin. Something, somewhere, wasn't right. The beam ricocheted off the small glass mirror above the children's chest of drawers and out the window.

It flashed through the village, then into the surrounding forest of pine and hemlock, flickering from icicle to icicle. Startling bats and surprising owls, it followed the old snow-covered Indian trail to the

Our heroic moonbeam

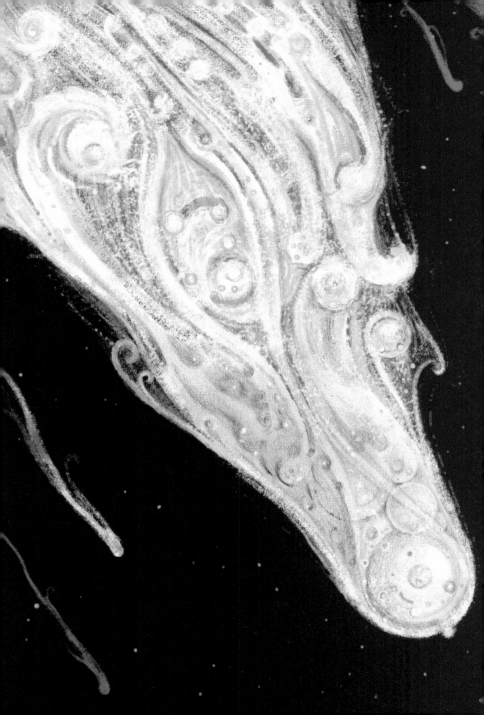

darkest part of the deep woods—a place the settlers feared and rarely ventured. Like a searchlight, the beam shot out into the darkness until it found a cave.

Strange rocks, curling like melted wax, framed the yawning mouth of the cavern. The cave was thick with shadows that seemed to breathe like living things. In all its travels, the beam had never seen anything so ominous.

The moonbeam wavered and then—not sure if it was being brave or foolish—dropped down, following the shadows into the pit below.

The darkness seemed to go on and on forever. Finally, the moonbeam came to a stagnant pool. Black water reflected its glow, dimly lighting the cave. And there, in the center of the pool, stood a giant figure. He was denser and even darker than the shadows that surrounded him. Still as a statue, he wore a long cloak as inky as an oil seep. The moonbeam scanned the figure slowly, cautiously. When it reached his eyes, they opened! The figure was awake!

The shadows began writhing about at the feet of the figure, their low drone filling the air. They grew, crashing against the cave walls like waves against a ragged jetty. But they weren't shadows at all! They were creatures—creatures that no child or Moon messenger had seen for centuries. And the moonbeam knew at once: It was surrounded by Fearlings and Nightmare Men—slaves of the Nightmare King!

The moonbeam paled and faltered. Perhaps it should have given up and fled back to the Moon. If it had, this story would never have been told. But the moonbeam did not flee. Inching closer, it realized that the phantom figure was the one all moonbeams had been taught to watch for: It was Pitch, the

King of Nightmares! He had been pierced through the heart, a diamond-like dagger holding him pinned against a mound of ebony marble. Warily, the moonbeam crept closer still, grazing against the weapon's crystal hilt.

But light does not go around crystal, it goes through it, and suddenly, the beam was sucked into the blade! Twisting from side to side, the moonbeam was pulled on a jagged course to the blade's tip. It was trapped, suspended in Pitch's frozen, glassy heart. Pitch's chest began to glow from within as the moonbeam ricocheted about in a frenzy, desperate to escape. It was terrifyingly cold there—colder even than the darkest regions of space. But the moonbeam was not alone. There, just beyond the edge of the blade, in the farthest recesses of the phantom figure's heart, it could see the spectral shape of a tiny elfin child curled tight. A boy?

Hesitantly, the beam illuminated the child's head.

That little ray of light was all it took; the spectral boy began to grow. He burst forth from Pitch's chest joyfully, free at last! The moonbeam was thrown from side to side as the boy, with one quick tug, wrenched the radiant dagger from the cold heart that had trapped him. Bearing the blade aloft, with the moonbeam still caught inside lighting the way, the boy shot like a rocket straight up and out of the cursed cave and into the starry night. By the time his feet hit the snowy ground, he looked every bit like a real boy, if a real boy could be carved out of mist and light and miraculously brought to life.

Freed from the dagger's impaling, Pitch began to grow as well, rising like a living tower of coal. Swelling to a monstrous size, he followed the boy's illuminated trail to the surface.

Looking wildly up at the sky, Pitch sniffed the air in ecstasy. With one shrug and a toss of his midnight cloak, he blotted out the Moon. He crouched down and dug his fingers into the earth, letting the scents of the surrounding forest reach into his searching brain. He was ravenous, overwhelmed by a fiery hunger that burned him from within.

Breathing deeply, he trolled the winter wind for the prize he coveted, the tender meal he had craved even beyond freedom all those endless years of imprisonment down below: the good dreams of innocent children. He would turn those dreams into nightmares—every last one—till every child on Earth lived in terror. For that's how Pitch intended to exact his revenge upon all those who had dared imprison him!

As glorious thoughts of revenge filled Pitch's

mind, they ignited around him a cloud of sulfurous black. The cloud seeped upward from the seemingly bottomless pit of the cave. From that vapor, hurtling in all directions at once, came the shadow creatures—the Fearlings and Nightmare Men—thousands of them, horrendously shrieking. Like giant bats, they glided over the forest and beyond, invading the dreams of all who slept nearby.

By now the moonbeam was frantic. It had found Pitch! The Evil One! It had to return to the Moon and report back to Tsar Lunar! But it remembered the sleeping children back in their cabin. What if the Fearlings went after them? How could the moonbeam help if it was still trapped inside the diamond dagger? The beam bucked and strained, guiding the boy, who skittered along, light as air, back through the town, back to the small

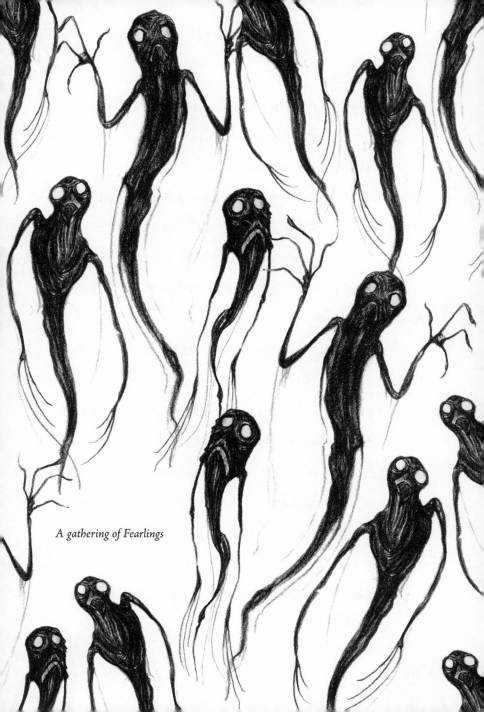

A gathering of Fearlings

children's window. They skidded to a stop.

The spectral boy pulled himself up onto the windowsill. As he peered in at the children, somewhere in his heart an ancient memory or remembrance stirred of a sleeping baby and a distant lullaby. But the memory dissolved almost as soon as it appeared, leaving him feeling deeply and unexpectedly sad.

Something dark flashed past the boy and into the children's room. Suddenly, two Fearlings hovered and twisted in midair above the sleeping brother and sister who turned restlessly, clutching at their quilts. Instinctually, the spectral boy leaped off the windowsill and snatched a broken tree branch from the ground, attaching the diamond dagger to its end. He aimed his gleaming weapon at the window.

The Fearlings shrunk back from the light, but they

did not disappear. So, for the second time that evening, the moonbeam glowed with all its might. The brightness was now too much for the Fearlings. With a low moan, they twined and curled, then vanished, as if they had never been there at all.

The children rolled over and nestled into their pillows with a smile.

And after seeing those smiles, the spectral boy laughed.

Up on the Moon, however, there was no cause for laughter. Tsar Lunar—the one we call the Man in the Moon—was on high alert. Something was amiss. Each night he sent thousands of moonbeams down to Earth. And each night they returned and made their reports. If they were still bright, all was well. But if they were darkened or tarnished from their travels,

Tsar Lunar would know that the children of Earth needed his help.

For a millennium all had been well and the moonbeams had returned as brightly as they had ventured forth. But now, one moonbeam had not returned.

And for the first time in a very long time, Tsar Lunar felt an ancient dread.

CHAPTER TWO

Wherein Speaking Insect Languages Proves to Be of Value

In THE FORESTED HINTERLANDS of eastern Siberia sat the little town of Santoff Claussen. There lived one of the last great wizards, Ombric Shalazar, and that morning, he was in deep discussion with a number of nocturnal insects, specifically a Lunar Moth, several fireflies, and a glowworm.

This was not unusual. Ombric could speak several thousand languages. He was fluent in the dialects of all manner of bugs, birds, and beasts; he could even speak hippopotamus.

As he switched from Lunar Moth to firefly, a group

of village children, early for school, hovered nearby. Many of them had just begun to learn some of the easier insect languages (ant, worm, snail), and though moth and firefly were difficult (glowworm, even more so), they could tell from the tone of the conversation that something was very wrong indeed.

Ombric was generally a wizard of extraordinary calm. Nothing seemed to surprise him. How could it? He was the last survivor of the lost city of Atlantis! He was a man who had seen and done everything. He could communicate telepathically to his owls. Walk through walls. Turn lead to gold. He'd helped invent time, gravity, and bouncing balls! But today, as he talked to this cluster of insects, he seemed, for the first time that the children had seen, perplexed and worried. His left eyebrow furrowed into a frown. Then suddenly, he turned to the children and said something he had never said before: "No lessons today. You should return to your homes—*now.*"

The children were amazed. Even disappointed. Lessons were *never* canceled and rarely over early! Sometimes they went on for so long that Ombric would have to stop time for a bit so they could go on even longer. This always caused great excitement because everything Ombric taught them was, without fail, fun. Not only did he show them how to make water flow backward and to properly dam a stream, he also taught them how to climb most everything, build catapults, and, best of all, the secrets of the imagination. "To understand pretending," Ombric was fond of saying, "is to conquer all barriers of time and space."

In fact, all of their studies were focused on how to make anything they thought of—no matter how impossible or fantastical—come true. And so, dejected and uneasy about the change to their daily routine, the children trudged back to their homes. Some lived in trees, some underground, some half and half. For Santoff Claussen was unlike any other village in the world. Every home had a secret passageway or trapdoor or magic room. Telescopes, and retractable roofs made of evergreen sprigs were the norm. That was how Ombric had dreamed it should be. He wanted a village that seemed impossible.

From the time Ombric was a very young wizard, he had journeyed to every corner of the Earth in search of the perfect place to create a haven for fellow dreamers. But it wasn't until he was nearly hit by a meteor (which, fortunately, exploded two hillsides over) that he found just the right spot. Barely acknowledging his close call, he had investigated the still-warm crater. There, at its exact center, was a

lone sapling that had survived the crash. The sapling glowed with what Ombric instantly deduced was the energy of ancient starlight.

The wizard tended the little tree, and it grew—faster than he ever thought possible—into a wonder of nature. A wonder of the cosmos! It grew to the exact size of Ombric's dream for it. And it formed its limbs, roots, and trunk so that Ombric could live inside. The first children to see the great tree had named it Big Root. And from this headquarters, Ombric welcomed all those with inquiring minds and kind hearts. Soon a small village sprang up. Ombric called it Santoff Claussen, an ancient phrase from Atlantis that meant "place of dreams."

The wizard labored daily to make Santoff Claussen a perfect haven for learning—an enlightened place where no one would laugh at anyone (young or old), who dreamed of what was possible . . . and impossible. And so inventors, scientists, artists, and visionaries from across the globe were drawn to his village.

Ombric knew that not everyone felt the same way about learning. Why, look at what they had done to poor Galileo in Italy when he'd dared to suggest that the Earth revolved around the sun! So Ombric designed layers of magical barriers, one inside the other, to protect his village, and, like the Great Wall of China, it took him centuries to build.

First, he cultivated an encircling hedge of bracken and vines to guard the heart of Santoff Claussen. The ground around the village, rich with stardust, proved to be a fertilizer like no other, so thick vines sprang up, spreading as Ombric directed. They twined and twisted into a nearly impenetrable hedge, a hundred feet high, barbed with thorns the length of spears.

In spite of the thorns, however, strangers more interested in rumors of treasure than in learning made their way to Santoff Claussen. Like most master wizards, Ombric could conjure up diamonds and gems of eye-popping splendor as he pleased. He used them in spells and elixirs. Once used, they lost their gleam and had no further value. Yet rumors of his untold wealth persisted. Indeed, there *was* treasure in Santoff Claussen! It was just not the sort the treasure seekers coveted.

Still, they came, the storied riches too enticing for treasure hunters to resist. But when they were met by an enraged wizard, they started new rumors. They called Ombric a heretic, a warlock, and worse. They said he had stolen the souls of the people of Santoff Claussen and should be burned at the stake.

So Ombric conjured a second ring of defense—a great black bear, the largest in all the Russias, whose courage and devotion were unquestioned. The bear would patrol to protect the village from anyone who might cause harm.

Then, on the outer rim, Ombric planted a third ring—majestic oaks, the largest in the world, whose huge roots could rise up and block the advance of any who tried to enter with evil intent. Ombric had to search through seven of his most ancient journals to find just the right enchantment to accomplish that feat!

And in case that was not enough to keep the intruders away, Ombric conjured up one more thing: a ghostly temptress with a beguiling smile. Adorned with what seemed like glittering gems, his Spirit of the Forest could lure visitors of an unkind or ignoble disposition to a particularly useful doom, turning them into stone, cursed forever to be a part of the village's defenses.

Ombric's efforts proved successful. Eventually, fewer and fewer villains came to Santoff Claussen, and the village was spoken about only in whispers by the outsiders who still remembered it was there. Haunted, they said. Bewitched. A mystery best left unsolved if you knew what was good for you.

Solving mysteries, however, was a favorite pastime of the villagers, the children especially. The one that had them most curious was how Ombric made his spells. They loved to visit him unannounced, hoping to catch him in the middle of inventing a new species of talking pig, or frogs who could shoot bows and arrows. Once there, they would listen to their teacher hold forth on any subject he happened to be investigating.

They inevitably gathered around Ombric's table, where they'd poke and prod at the noisy gizmos and gadgets, bubbling vials of startling colors and shapes, globes of worlds known and unknown, clocks that could bend time, tools of bizarre and delightful functions, winged wind machines, weather manipulators, and magnifying lenses so powerful that they could see the secret writings of germs and microbes. And the books. Countless books. Mountains of books containing knowledge from the beginning of recorded time.

The children loved hearing about the singing mermaids from the island of Zanzibar. About the pirates of the Yangtze River. About the giant "Abominables"—furry snowmen who roamed the mountain ranges near the top of the world.

But that morning, when Ombric returned from

his talk with his insect friends, he needed to be alone in his study. There could be no children in Big Root today. He pulled the most ancient volumes from his library and read them intently. Silently. And with a frown. The insects had told him of things they had seen—disturbing things—in *his* enchanted forest! Shadows had come, cast from nothing that could be seen. Silent shadows in strange shapes. And they were coming deeper into the woods each night, closer and closer to Big Root.

CHAPTER THREE

A Terrifying Walk in the Woods

Ombric continued to study and worry in his Big Root lab until the first fireflies began to glow. An ancient evil was coming, he was sure, but he still had no plan or potion to fight it. However, Ombric was comforted in knowing he had some time to contemplate, for life all around him was unfolding as usual. Evenings in Santoff Claussen were not like those in other villages. For most villages, twilight signaled the day's end, the time to close down shop. But here, telescopes were being erected, experiments put into place, the bustle of busy minds filled the air. Children peppered their parents with questions: "Can a dream be captured? If we dream of flying, do we actually fly? Do toys come to life at night when no one is watching?" Boundless possibilites were explored, at least until the children had to be home.

The children were wily, even brilliant, at avoiding that dreaded span of the day called "bedtime." It was the one nearly impossible task the village faced each and every night. One night the children disguised themselves as statues. Another, they figured out how to hide inside the paintings on the walls. Most often they'd simply duck into the forest, where even the bear would sometimes hide them. And the herd of Great Reindeer was clearly in on the game, for many were the evenings when they would gallop between the trees with the laughing children on their backs, just ahead of their pursuing parents.

Child traps were finally invented, intended to shorten the nightly ritual. Gently but firmly, the traps would catch the children, wash them, brush their teeth, clothe them in the proper pajamas, and catapult them to their bedrooms.

But the children were getting better at avoiding these traps. So the nightly struggle grew more complex. It was a game that the parents indulged and Ombric always enjoyed, but there were times when patience would wear thin. Once, the children even stood in plain sight atop the trees that ringed the village, but, having painted themselves with sky and stars—with Ombric's magical paints, no less!—they were not discovered until dawn.

On this particular evening, however, things were decidedly different. The children were tired, they said. Ready for bed, they said. They *wanted* to sleep.

Early, even! The parents were unsure if this was a gift, a trick, or some sort of epidemic. Being parents, though—and tired of the nightly struggle—they gratefully went along. For once they would enjoy an early tucking in.

But a childwide plot was afoot, and it worked perfectly. When their parents were sound asleep, the children snuck from their homes, made their way past Big Root undetected, and ran to the enchanted woods. For they had also spoken to the ants and slugs (slug merely being a variant of the worm dialect) after Ombric had sent them from his laboratory. What the slugs and ants had to say was difficult to understand since the words "infiltrated" and "unfamiliar" were hard to translate. One girl, the gray-eyed Katherine, the only child who was being raised by Ombric and who actually lived in Big Root, had the best grasp of the conversation.

"There's something new and strange in the forest," she told the others. The insects weren't sure what it was. The question of whether these invaders would turn out to be good or evil hadn't entered the children's minds. They were just doing as they had been taught: to be curious. So lanterns in hand, they set out, eager to discover their new mysterious guests.

The children ventured deeper and deeper into the forest, following the familiar trails. Not an owl nor chipmunk greeted them. No skunk said hello. They couldn't even hear the bear, whose rumble of walking or snoring was always a reassuring sound. Everything was oddly quiet. Moonlight barely pierced the thick canopy of limbs and vines.

The children glanced at one another nervously. No one wanted to be the first to suggest turning back.

Ombric called them his "hale and hearty daredevils."
How could they turn back?

But then the air itself grew unnaturally still
and for the first time, the children felt afraid. They
huddled against one another and watched the dark
grow darker. And then they, too, fell silent.

The first scream didn't come till the Fearlings had
almost reached them.

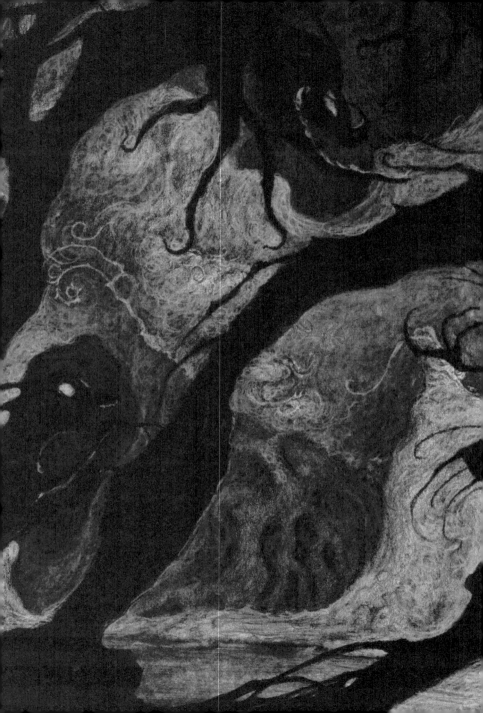

CHAPTER FOUR

Out of the Shadows
Come Deeper Mysteries

THE SHADOWS MOVED SLOWLY, soundlessly, encircling the children, drawing closer and closer with each rotation.

The children bunched together as tightly as they could. At first they had screamed, but that had only made the shadows come nearer, so they had again fallen silent. They watched one another's faces stiffen with fear in the dim lantern light. How could they defend themselves against these unnatural *things?* What would Ombric have done?

The eldest boy, Tall William, the first son of Old

William, opened the vent in his lantern and held it high. But the spidery shadows grew longer, reaching for the mass of children even more menacingly, as if challenging the light. "I thought that would help," he said, puzzled, trying to sound brave. He closed the lantern's vents.

"Perhaps if we run," suggested another boy.

"No!" cried Katherine. "We must stay together. Look! Something's coming!" She pointed to tiny lights that were beginning to dot the forest around them. Fireflies! In numbers too vast to calculate, they swarmed forth and attacked the shadows like luminous darts released from an invisible bow. Moments later the birds, the reindeer, and nearly every creature in the forest joined them! Then the trees began to swing their branches; the vines lashed out like whips. But how can a shadow be fought?

The shadows splintered apart. But since they were shadows, they instantly came together again, taking new forms. They snapped and crushed the vines and hurled the forest defenders as if they were leaves in the wind. Undaunted, the forest army fought desperately on, rising repeatedly to protect the children. Still, the shadows slipped past them and began to envelop the children in a blanket of darkness. The older children immediately draped themselves over the younger ones in a last effort to protect them. *And where is the bear? Surely the bear will help us*, they thought as the inky blackness flooded over them.

Then out of the night sped something swift and bright—something that moved almost too quickly to be seen. It was brighter than fire, and the shadows cowered. And then there was laughter. The bright laughter of mischief.

And in a single perfect moment the children saw what looked to be a spritelike boy holding a staff with a brilliant moonlit glow at its end. He seemed to glisten like beads of light. He stood calmly amidst the chaos, his laughter bringing forth swirls of mist that hovered in the air. Then, in an instant, he blurred into a hundred shafts of refracting light that came together around the children like a protective cone, driving back the shadowy blanket. Then he blistered out in all directions, driving back every shadowy creature that could be seen.

When the shadows vanished, so did the spectral boy, leaving behind only a breeze of misty laughter that drifted over the woods like an echo.

The children stood up slowly. The forest creatures righted themselves. As the boys and girls looked around in stunned disbelief, they saw their parents and Ombric approaching from the edge of the forest. For once, in this town where surprise was the order of the day, no one knew quite what to say about what they had just seen. Even Ombric was rendered momentarily speechless. But the wizard now understood what they were all about to face.

"I suggest, given current events, that the safest place for the children to sleep this night is Big Root," he said finally. "An ancient evil has awakened—and I must tell you more. Come."

And before anyone could agree or not, the wizard threw open his cloak and transported them all to the tree.

CHAPTER FIVE

The Golden Age

FOR SUCH AN OTHERWORLDLY fellow, Ombric was a very thoughtful host. Not only had he brought everyone in the village to his tree, but with a quiet command, he asked Big Root to form sleeping quarters for all the children, and the tree complied, as it always did, with his wishes. Bunk beds materialized from its hollow center, fanning out like the spokes of a giant wheel. Each row was stacked five beds high. And twisting down the center was a spiral staircase.

Cookies, chocolates, and warm cocoa hovered in the air by each bed. The fear ebbed from the children as they reached for the sweets. The adults were more wary. They knew these treats were meant to comfort. So they were braced. . . . What was Ombric going to tell them?

While the children delighted in which type of cookie they'd received, Ombric stood at the bottom of the stairs, looking up pensively at the high hollow of Big Root. He raised one finger skyward and twirled it in a circular motion. From the top of the tree's hollow, bark began to peel back until a large round portal, like a window, opened up.

The whole village was there, parents and grandparents, aunts and uncles. The children leaned out from their bunks. They could now see up to the starry sky and the Moon, glowing bright and beautiful.

"Tonight we find ourselves at the center of an ancient war," Ombric began, walking slowly up the staircase. "Look at our Moon. It was not always there to light our night. A war brought it to us—a war with the Nightmare King." He paused and waved his arm toward the glowing sphere.

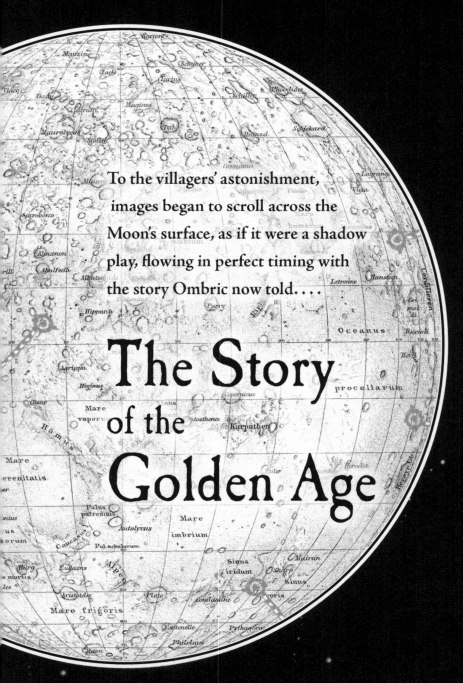

To the villagers' astonishment,
images began to scroll across the
Moon's surface, as if it were a shadow
play, flowing in perfect timing with
the story Ombric now told. . . .

The Story
of the
Golden Age

There once was a time called the Golden Age.
It is said that there has never been anything
as magnificent before or since. Travel among the
planets and stars was common then. The galaxies
were filled with airships of every size and shape
imaginable. And the universe was ruled by the
Constellations—groups of stars and planets led
by great, benevolent families who governed with
imagination, fairness, and flair. Of these regal
families, the House of Lunanoff was most beloved;
if the Golden Age had true royalty, it was Tsar
and Tsarina Lunanoff.

Early on, however, the Seas of Space were rife with treacherous bands of outlaws: Fearlings, Nightmare Men, Dream Pirates. The Lunanoffs had pledged to rid all evil from the Golden Age, and together with the other Constellations, they built a prison out of lead in the farthermost regions of space. There, they entombed the criminals of the cosmos in eternal darkness until they became little more than shadows. And the Golden Age flourished.

But darkness came in the shifting shape of a villain named Pitch. Pitch had been the Age's greatest hero. He had led the Golden Armies in capturing the Fearlings and their ilk. And when all the evil had been rooted out, he valiantly volunteered to guard the prison's single entrance. The Constellations agreed, for with Pitch on watch, no nightmarish prisoner would ever escape.

But evil is a cunning force. It can find the

weakness in any man, even the bravest. For years
Pitch listened to the constant whispered chatter
of the prisoners pleading through the door. "One
breath of fresh air. Please," they hissed. "One small
breeze."

It only takes a single weak moment to let evil
in . . . or out. And one day Pitch opened the door.
Just to let in some air.

That was all it took.

The evil shadows rushed out and engulfed
Pitch. They poured into him, possessing him
utterly until they darkened his soul
forever. From that moment on,
he was a madman—his strength
and abilities increased tenfold,
and his heart, once noble, was
now cold and cruel. His mind
was twisted with the shadows'

thoughts of vengeance. He would destroy the House of Lunanoff. He would end the Golden Age he had once loved and defended. And he would do it by turning all good dreams into nightmares.

With his shadowy Nightmare Men and Fearlings, Pitch sailed the heavens on waves of fear, plundering planets, extinguishing stars, and scuttling any airship that crossed his path, savagely stealing every dream and replacing it with misery and despair. The dreams he hungered for most were those of children—the pure of heart. He could sense children from seven planets off, and with a mere touch of his hand, he could leave them plagued with nightmares for the rest of their lives. And for some there was a worse fate. Pitch turned some children into Fearlings, glorying in their pathetic moans and cries as he transformed them from humans to dark phantoms.

Pitch had ravaged every outpost of the Golden Age, except the Constellation Lunanoff. He had saved the best for last. For the Lunanoffs had a child. A son. Not just a son, a prince. Prince Lunar. And the prince had never had a nightmare!

For that youngest Lunanoff, Pitch had a special fate planned. The Nightmare King would make him one of his own. No lowly Fearling would Prince Lunar be. Instead, he would be the Prince of Nightmares!

And so the hunt began. The Lunanoffs knew that Pitch would come for them. They had constructed a remarkable craft called the *Moon Clipper* that was not only the swiftest ship in the galaxies but, with the flick of a switch, could transform itself into a Moon. The Lunanoffs were at full sail toward a distant galaxy with their stalwart crew of Moonbots. Their destination: a small, uncharted green and blue planet known only to them. It was called Earth. In those days Earth had no Moon, which made it a perfect destination. If Pitch came near, they would go into hiding, disguised as a Moon.

But despite the Lunanoffs' best efforts, Pitch had spotted them. He attacked just as they neared the small planet. It was the last great battle of the Golden Age and unlike any the galaxies had ever seen, for Tsar and Tsarina Lunanoff would die rather than have Pitch take their child. The crew, too, was ready to fight to the last, and they knew the secret of how to fight a shadow. Meteors or shooting

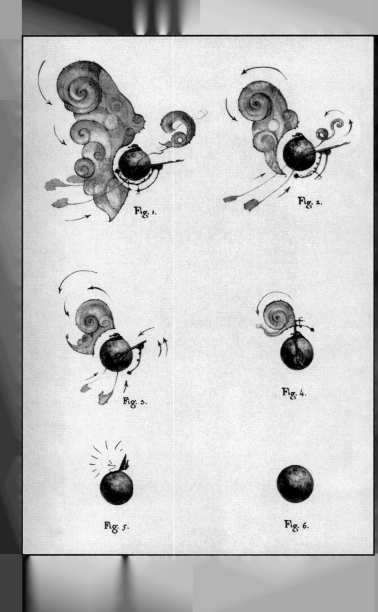

Fig. 1.

Fig. 2.

Fig. 3.

Fig. 4.

Fig. 5.

Fig. 6.

stars carved and fashioned into swords, spears, and bombs were filled with an astral brightness that shadows could not withstand.

Though the Lunanoffs heroically defended the *Moon Clipper*, the outer hull of their craft was blasted and battered until its guns were too damaged to fire. Then Pitch, with his innumerable phantoms, were able to overwhelm the *Moon Clipper*. Just as they captured Tsar and Tsarina Lunanoff, there was a great explosion—brighter than twenty suns. The cause of that explosion has never been known. Who or what stopped Pitch is one of the greatest mysteries of the Golden Age.

Pitch and his Fearlings were never seen again. Nor were the young prince's parents. And the *Moon Clipper* would nevermore set sail. It would rotate forever around the Earth—by all appearances, a lifeless rock.

And what became of the baby prince? His parents had sequestered him during the battle, deep in one of the Moon's many hollow chambers.

The prince survived, as did a small contingent of Moonbots and other Moon creatures. But Prince Lunar was no longer a prince. He was now the new Tsar Lunar, the only surviving member of the House of Lunanoff. The Moonbots' devotion to the young tsar was unflagging, and they did everything in their power to make up for the loneliness he felt without his parents. He was doted upon and indulged. With the entire Moon as his playground, his life was a never-ending series of wild, hurtling, do-as-you-please days. There were tunnels to explore. Craters to slide down. Mountaintop jumping (a benefit of little gravity).

There was no school, no schedule, no bedtime, no real rules. But the planet became his school by virtue of its wonders. He learned to use the

battalions of telescopes his parents had secreted in the hidden caves of the *Moon Clipper*. He began to observe the nearby Earth and its people. This became one of his favorite pastimes—watching the Earthling families, who were so much like his own had been. Knowing that others were close gave him comfort and lessened his loneliness.

As he grew, the young tsar came to look upon the children of Earth as his friends, and he began to send them dreams, using machines that had been developed during the height of the Golden Age and were still aboard the *Moon Clipper*. And the Earth began to flourish as never before.

But Tsar Lunar always keeps watch, wary that someday Pitch may somehow return and destroy the new Golden Age he hoped would begin on our Earth.

Here Ombric stopped his story. The images on the Moon faded away. The villagers turned to the wizard.

"Pitch has returned," said Ombric evenly. "We've seen the proof." He pulled a small glass jar from his cloak. Inside was a fist-size Fearling, churning and desperate to escape. A chorus of worried gasps came from the children and their parents.

"It can't get out," Ombric assured them. "The glass is made from star sand, like the windows in Big Root."

Everyone nodded with relief. Then a flood of questions sounded out.

"But are we safe?" asked one parent.

"Will they return?"

"How do we fight them?"

"Are you powerful enough to stop them?"

"Who was that boy with the staff?"

"You can see the future! Tell us!"

Ombric held up his hand to quiet them. He looked at his friends with ancient eyes, his brow furrowed deeply. "It is true, I know many things," he said. "But this is beyond even my abilities. I am certain of only this: We are strong. We are brave. But we will need help. The children will sleep here tonight where they are safest."

Then he opened the Fearling's jar. The creature streaked out and flew about the room, swirling and diving through the bunks. The children ducked under the covers as it neared. Their parents reached out to protect them, glancing at one another nervously. The next instant, a moonbeam shined down from the Moon and chased after the Fearling. Light is quicker than shadow so the beam easily caught the Fearling, and with one touch, the awful creature dissolved into nothingness.

As the room calmed, Ombric approached this new moonbeam. "Did Lunar send that glowing boy?" he asked with urgency in his voice. The children grinned at one another. Of course Ombric spoke the language of moonbeams! The beam dimmed and its light flickered. Ombric nodded. "No? Most interesting." He stroked his eyebrows. "Now return to your home, young soldier," he told the moonbeam. "Tell Tsar Lunar what you've seen. Send what help you can." The moonbeam paused for a moment and then shot back up through Big Root's open hollow, into the sky.

"Will it help us?" asked a boy named Fog.

"I have every hope," replied Ombric.

"I don't want to have nightmares," cried Fog's sister.

"Will I be turned into a Fearling?" asked Katherine, who sat in her usual bed.

Ombric turned to Katherine. He'd cared for her since she was a baby, so she held a special place in his heart. "Not as long as there is breath in this old wizard!" Then lowering his eyebrows to their usual calm position, he twirled a single finger to shut the portal at the top of Big Root's hollow and bade the parents good night. The most they could do was try to get some sleep. But in the darkest part of the night, sleep was shattered. A terrible, ground-trembling, ferocious roar sounded out through Santoff Claussen.

CHAPTER SIX

Nicholas St. North
(A Most Unlikely Source of Help)

LATER THAT NIGHT, IN the raggedy camp of the wildest ruffians of the Russian plains, there slept a young bandit chief named Nicholas St. North. No one knew exactly how old he was, for even he did not know his birthday, but he was old enough for the beginnings of a beard and was without argument the most daring young rascal in all the Russias. A hero he was not. But it was said that he once defeated an entire regiment of cavalry with a bent steak knife—while he was eating. Impressive swordsmanship indeed, but not the kind of achievement that would make a mother proud.

North had no mother or father or family that he could remember. He had never been tucked into bed. He'd never known the safety of a home or the tenderness of a mother's embrace, nor the happy camaraderie of a father's company. His boyhood was spent in the wilds, aware of himself only as both predator and prey. There are skills that develop when one grows up forgotten and wild: keen eyes, light steps, impossible quickness. These skills would become North's native tongue—that and a preternatural sense of where danger lies. As a boy, he fled from that feeling, but as he grew older he pursued it.

Trees produce growth rings for each birthday, but North had no way to mark the time that had passed. He was somewhere in his teens, though, when he was taken in by the Cossacks, the most savage tribe of warriors in the Russian Empire. Soon North became their greatest fighter. With dirk, dagger, or pistol, he was matchless. They taught him their language. And then he charmed them out of rations, supplies, and common sense. It would be logical to assume that a taste of civility (if one can call the Cossacks "civil") would tame the lad, but North remained just as wild—only now, having learned from these warriors, he was more cunning, powerful, and well fed.

Still, along with all these dubious qualities, there came a ready smile. "Life is made up of danger and heartbreak," he'd boast. "I laugh in the face of both!" Yet for all his humor and charm, North thought of no one but himself, caring only for the thrill of battle and the pursuit of treasure. But Cossacks were, at heart, a cruel bunch, and North, even with his meager moral outlook, could not abide their disregard for human life.

And so he had left the Cossack brotherhood to become a bandit—the most notorious in Europe. Never caught and always at the ready, he and his ragtag band of outlaws had plundered half the wealth of the continent. But the money never lasted long. They gambled and wasted it away almost as quickly as they stole it.

North was, in fact, sound asleep and dreaming of just how to steal the other half of the continent's riches when a moonbeam, sent by the Man in the Moon himself, shined down into the bandits' camp. It darted from outlaw to outlaw, flickering to the ear of Sergei the Terrible. Nope, wrong thief. Putin the Creepy. Not right either. Then Gregor of the Mighty Stink. Yikes! Wrong again. Then, finally, it found North. Ah yes, the bandit prince! In perfect Russian, the moonbeam began to transmit the message,

North's strange departure. Then one by one, they rose up, mounted their own horses, and rode into the black night after their leader. Dark it may have been. Certainly too dark to see. But that didn't matter. They could still hear the laughter. And they knew by its tone that Nicholas St. North was leading them to adventure and riches beyond anything they'd ever dreamed of.

North has a two-shot dream.

CHAPTER SEVEN

Is Not Really a Chapter at All—Just a Piece of the Greater Puzzle

ON A CRAGGY MOUNTAINTOP high above the Russian wilderness, that boy, that spectral boy who braved the Fearlings and shadows, hid from the moonlight. He peeked out from between boulders left behind by ancient glaciers, then instantly hunkered back into the darkness. The Moon knew he was there. A handful of moonbeams danced about the rocks as if teasing him out. The boy peeked again, drew back, then couldn't resist one more look. The beams bounced from rock to rock, and slowly, hesitantly, the boy stepped forward into the light and gazed up at the Moon.

For once, he stood perfectly still, staring intently at the Moon's glowing orb. He began to recognize the face—a face from long ago. It was the face of his oldest and dearest friend, whom he had not seen since the fateful battle with Pitch. Dozens, then hundreds, of moonbeams shined down and danced around the boy. The wind began to pick up, and misty mountain clouds swirled by him, not but an arm's length away. The moonbeams started to strobe and flicker.

The beam trapped inside the boy's diamond-tipped staff flashed excitedly. The staff began to shake in the boy's hand. He brought it to his face and looked closely at the beam. It seemed to speak to him. He instinctively raised the staff to the sky. The moonbeams around him then focused on the diamond. In fevered bursts of light, they appeared to celebrate the finding of their lost comrade. Messages were apparently being sent and received, then the staff pulled the boy toward the passing clouds. As a brilliant glow filled the air, the boy stepped right off the edge of the mountain peak. But he did not fall! As his foot reached the open air, it landed upon one of the clouds that was soaring by.

The spectral boy took one step, then another. He looked down around himself. He was standing on a cloud!

The next instant, he was running, bounding from cloud to cloud, faster than seemed possible. He was smiling, as no boy, spectral or otherwise, has ever smiled before.

CHAPTER EIGHT

Where the Impossible Occurs with Surprising Regularity

NICHOLAS ST. NORTH AND his men rode all night, but it was a most unnatural evening. North's laughter had finally subsided, but still he charged relentlessly south, like a cheerful madman. The Moon seemed to light the way for them, leading them through the darkest gorges and densest forests.

After several hours at a hard gallop, they came to a river that was too swift to cross. Before the bandits could even slow down, they saw a streaking figure— Was it a boy? Made of light? There followed a dazzling flash that illuminated the water in a strange, otherworldly way. North peered at the river, his instincts kicking in. He was a betting lad, after all, and he sensed that these moonbeams were coaxing him to trust in the impossible. With a nudge, he urged Petrov forward, and they strode right onto the river. They did not sink but rode atop the water! North's men dashed after them. It was like that again and again. Lakes, streams, fjords—any body of water that blocked their path would light up and magically support them.

And then, as they climbed high into the mountains, something even more astounding occurred. At the edge of a steep escarpment, the mountain sheared off into nothingness. North pulled on Petrov's reins; the horse reared back just in time to avoid a plummeting drop. North surveyed the edge—below them was nothing but clouds. If they pressed ahead, they'd fall. There was no telling how far, but it was certain death.

Then there it was again—that glowing boy, the burst of light coursing through the clouds! And yet again North laughed out loud. He cracked Petrov's reins and they raced forward. Before his men could shout for him to stop, he'd hurtled off the edge. North and Petrov fell a few feet, then landed on a cloud. They rode on, North now laughing with a reckless joy.

Stunned, his men soared after him, and they, too, began to laugh at the wild, fantastic folly of what they knew was impossible, and yet there it was happening. On and on they rode through these new cloud mountains and valleys, across the white glistening landscape of the air.

CHAPTER NINE
The Battle of the Bear

THE ENCHANTED CLOUDS SLOPED past the high hills just outside of Santoff Claussen. North and his men skidded down the last cloud's wavy edge and jumped to the solid ground just below.

Dawn was breaking; the sky was just beginning to brighten with hints of purple and blue.

North barreled forward, urging Petrov toward a dense wooded grove that he suspected surrounded a village. For it was this village he was headed toward, the village called Santoff Claussen, as he'd explained to his men as they'd thundered through the night. "Riches, lads!" he'd bellowed out. "I saw it all in a dream. Treasures like we've never seen—not by a half! Not by a tenth! And they're ours to find!" He'd warned they'd be tested: "Vines with thorns that can cut you in two; trees with roots like lashes. A bear thirty feet tall!"

One of his men shouted out, "But, Captain, no bandit has ever faced those defenses and lived!"

North let out a great "Ha!" He paused only for an instant. "*WE* are no ordinary bandits!" Then he cracked his leather crop and stormed onward.

Now, just ahead of the sun, the men quickened toward the row of titanic oaks that lined the outer edge of the forest, their huge roots rising up and blocking any path inside. North did not flinch. With Petrov at a full gallop, he rode straight at them. At the last moment the mountainous roots groaned to life. They arched and shifted like prehistoric serpents, forming an entrance large enough for North and his men to ride through. North was sure this was a sign. *The village's defenses are already surrendering!* he thought. *Perhaps the defenses know exactly who they are up against!* "The forest fears us, lads!" he crowed. With whip and spur, they galloped on.

They rushed through the vast, heaving tumult of tree roots, then hurtled into a barbed tangle of giant vines. The vines untwined their centuries of knotting and let them pass. North glanced at the retreating vines' spearlike thorns with disdain—this was almost too easy! He grinned back triumphantly at his men. *Now, bring on the bear.*

The first streams of sunlight began to flicker through the fortress of limbs and tree trunks. North could make out the tracings of a well-worn trail and, farther ahead, the open knolls of the village. He raised an arm, urging his men onward, when a terrifying roar shattered the early morning quiet. The bear! The roar echoed out again, louder, closer. North drew his sword and rose up in his saddle, eager to see the beast. His men followed suit. So there was going to be a fight after all!

But as they rounded a bend in the path, it was not a bear they saw at all. Blocking their way was a beautiful misty figure—Ombric's last line of defense, the Spirit of the Forest. Her shimmering veils, laced with tiny gemstones, shifted and floated around her, as if moving to a breeze that only she could feel. The men reined in their horses and glanced at one another. Not even North's dream had told of this creature. The Spirit beckoned them closer. As they neared, her eyes glowed and glistened, greener than the emeralds they'd once stolen from the sultan of Constantinople. She seemed made of jewels—the most extraordinary they had ever seen. This must be the fabled treasure!

Though the bear's bellows continued, the thieves heard only the jangling of the Spirit's bracelets. North's men began to dismount their horses, mesmerized. They walked toward her, lowering their swords. But North was unsure. He looked in the direction of the bear's roar, then back. A shaft of dawn's light illuminated the Spirit, and her radiance was now blinding. Feeling hypnotized, even North could no longer pull his gaze from her. The world around him seemed to fall away as he imagined the treasure she must surely be guarding. She reached a pale hand toward him, then opened her slender fingers—gold! North began to lower his saber, ignoring Petrov, who was shaking his mane in frustration.

The Spirit looked into North's eyes. She drifted forward, holding the gold coins higher. Then she held out both hands—thousands of coins were spilling to the ground. The treasure was there before him. He need only take it. He *wanted* to take it. But Petrov reared up and slammed his hooves against the ground. Suddenly North could hear screaming from the village. He tore his eyes from the spirit—the roar of the bear and the panicked screaming flooding his ears. The screams were coming from children! It sounded as if . . . they were screaming for their lives! The sound pulled at North's soul, reached into a place in his heart he did not know existed. And for the first time in his life, he turned away from treasure.

He snatched up Petrov's reins and wheeled away from the glittering phantom. "Lads! This way!" he barked, but they were transfixed. Slapping the reins against Petrov's neck, North shot his men one last look, just in time to see them scrambling after the loose coins. To his horror, the moment their fingers grasped the coins, they turned to stone. Dashing bandits no longer, they froze into hunched, hideous trolls and elves.

Before North could fathom what this meant, he heard the children's cries again. As in all moments of true bravery, North's heart beat so strongly that it filled his whole body with a steady, urgent pulse, flooding his head until there was no thinking, just action. The pounding of his heart was echoed by the drumming of Petrov's hooves as North raced toward the screams. A second chorus of screams rose up, and North urged Petrov even faster.

But when they reached the town center, Petrov reared back. The scene before them was like something out of a nightmare. North had seen many things, but nothing in his young life to match this. A tree, an oak of staggering size, was actually fighting an enormous black bear. His muscles, dense and flexed with aggression, rippled under an endless mass of fur. The tree's roots had torn from the ground and were thrashing and grabbing at the bear like an octopus. It swung a massive limb to strike at the bear, but the creature blocked the blow, snapping the branch off at the trunk and sending it crashing into a house. Then the bear clawed at the tree's trunk, digging holes that revealed the tree's hollow.

It was there, *inside* the tree, where North saw the children, at least a dozen of them, cowering and terrified. In front of them stood an ancient wizard madly waving a wooden staff, shouting what sounded like the beginnings of an incantation. But before the wizard could finish, the bear shredded away a huge swathe of bark and snatched the wizard from the hollow, gulping him down in one ferocious bite. The children burrowed deeper into the farthest notches of the tree, quivering.

The tree gave a great shudder, then its roots and limbs fell limp. The bear sprang free. He eyed the children and raised a massive paw. But North had begun his charge. He had the advantage—he saw the bear, but the bear had not yet seen him! He rammed Petrov into the bear's black fur at full speed, knocking the brutish creature off balance. Drawing a second saber, North managed a half dozen deep wounds before the bear regained his footing. With a roar that shook the forest, the creature swung around faster than North ever thought possible. One single swipe was enough to fling thief and horse into the air. North landed in the tree's hollow. Though badly wounded, he did not falter. With the children huddled behind him, he stood his ground.

"Our bear has gone mad!" one of the children told him breathlessly.

"Our Ombric," came the teary voice of a young girl, "has been eaten!" She choked on the words, struggling, he could tell, to contain a sob.

"Then he'll eat no more," replied North, and braced for the bear's attack.

The bear rose to his full height, casting a shadow over the bandit and the children. His claws were ready. His teeth were bared. He let out a growl so low and ominous, North could feel it in his bones.

For once, North did not laugh in the face of danger.

With blinding speed, he threw six daggers, three from each hand, and riddled the bear with knives.

Then he redrew his sabers and attacked. The bear struck back. But North was at the ready. In an instant he'd sliced off the deadly tips of the bear's claws. The bear surged forward; North, both sabers in hand, plunged.

Rare two-handed Polish Keep Sweeper

But the bear was not done. He tossed North to the ground like a rag doll. The bandit, stunned, could not get up. The bear lunged at him, his full weight bearing down. But North was not finished either. He would not let that monster have the children. With what little strength he had left, he raised both sabers just as the beast's massive body slammed on top of him.

The bear landed with the violence of a meteorite.

The ground shook for miles. A cloud of dirt and earth mushroomed up, turning the morning sky ashen.

In the silence that followed, the children looked out from the splintered gashes of Big Root. They could just make out the bear's huge shape through the haze of dust. He shifted and lurched, trying to get to his feet. His breathing was labored and short. With one long, mournful groan, he slowly rolled over and moved no more.

As the air began to clear, the children gasped. The man with the swords lay on the bear's chest. Both sabers were jammed to the hilt in the black fur just above the behemoth's heart. The man lay unmoving as well; he looked so small and ragged, like a toy. In a daze the children crept forward to stare at the valiant swordsman. Their world was shattered. Their beloved bear had turned into a monster and destroyed everything they held dear. But they wanted, somehow, to help this man who had so courageously saved them. Ombric would know what to do, but Ombric . . .

Some of the children began to cry softly. Others kneeled, reaching out to touch the crumpled man. And as they did so, a dark, shadowy mist began to rise up from the mouth of the bear. An inky mass began to form. It grew larger, sizzling and writhing in the morning light. Then it sharpened into a shape that towered above them. The children drew back. They'd seen this face before—in the story Ombric had showed them of the Golden Age.

Looking down on them was Pitch himself. In his hands was Ombric's carved staff, broken in two. "This is all that's left of your precious wizard," he sneered.

CHAPTER TEN

In Which a Great Many Things Occur Swiftly

WITH NO ONE TO protect them, the children were certain they were doomed. Pitch leaned down closer. The children backed away. His face! His awful face was a nightmare in itself—not so much ugly as haunted, cold, without a hint of kindness. Centuries of cruelty reflected from his piercing stare. Yet there was a magnificence about him like that of an approaching storm. The children had never beheld any being that seemed so powerful. Not Ombric. Not their bear. They were frozen in a sort of mesmerized, terrible awe.

Pitch leaned closer still, but as he did so, the children noticed something. Pitch seemed to be fading, growing dimmer as the morning sun reached past the trees. And then dimmer still. The children could barely believe what was happening. They didn't dare move.

"In time . . . ," Pitch whispered, wincing in the sunlight, "in time you'll be mine."

And in eerie silence Pitch began to seep slowly into the ground. He tried desperately to hold on to the two halves of Ombric's staff, but as he became more and more translucent, the pieces slipped through his hands and fell to the grass. Then, in a dank, smoky mist, Pitch dissolved into the earth until there was no trace of him at all.

The terror gone, the children scrambled out of the remains of Big Root. They looked about wildly, and there, running toward them, flooding around them, enveloping them in their arms, were their parents.

"You're safe, you're safe!" one mother called out, tears falling onto the head of the small boy she clutched.

"I'm so sorry," cried a father. "He trapped us in our sleep!"

"We could hear your cries, but we couldn't move," murmured another mother, hugging her little girl tightly.

"Something happened to our bear!" the tallest boy told them.

"Ombric's been eaten!" another boy sobbed.

"That man saved us! And he's been killed!" a girl hiccupped, pressing her face into her father's chest.

"But you're safe, you're safe," the parents said again and again, and the joy of that started to turn sobs to smiles, wails to grins.

Only little Katherine stood apart, pressing her lips together until they were pale. Then, with a slight tilt of her head, she left the group to join Old William, the village elder. He stood over the place where Pitch had vanished. Only a small crack in the hardened dirt remained. He looked at the bear and the fallen hero who had defended the children. The old man shook his head. His was a sadness that was just beginning to sink in.

Katherine took his hand, and soon one, then another, of the villagers trickled over. They looked at the broken pieces of Ombric's staff. "How can this be?" whispered Old William.

And the joyful clamor of reuniting families began to give way to piercing grief. Some of the children started to lean against the bear's unmoving body, clasping and hugging his thick, black fur.

"No! Don't touch him!" cried Fog's father, pulling Fog away.

Tears welled in the child's eyes. "But he's our bear!"

Another child chimed in, "He'd never hurt us on purpose!"

"It wasn't his fault. That bad one changed him," said Katherine. "Think of what he's been to us!"

Then everyone stopped and remembered. Not the bear's last terrifying moments of madness, but the years of devotion and friendship. The way he had protected them time and again. And what of Ombric? Big Root? Were they lost forever?

The sorrow began to spread. First, the trees ringing the outer rim of the village began to sway, their limbs sinking toward the forest floor. Then the rest of the forest followed—every inhabitant, be it plant, insect, or animal, flooding the air with a heavy, woeful roll of sound, as if the entire world were moaning. The sky darkened. The wind began to swell. Leaves began to snap away from the trees, the vines, and the bushes. Big Root was stripped of all its foliage, the swirling leaves circling around Santoff Claussen like a tempest of tears. Through the blur, the villagers could see something moving toward them.

It was the Spirit of the Forest. She glided to them and hovered over Ombric's broken staff. She too was weeping, her jewels now dull, her tears falling on the staff's broken edges.

The village would never be the same. That seemed certain. But Ombric's first lesson to anyone who lived in Santoff Claussen was simple: There's a little bit of wizard in everyone. That magic's real power was in belief. That every spell began, "I believe. I believe. I believe." Old William picked up the two halves of Ombric's staff and fit them back together precisely along the break. He looked at Katherine intently. She instantly understood.

"Ombric's first lesson," she whispered. She ran her fingers along the break, smoothing the splinters down into the staff. "I believe. I believe. I believe," she said. The deafening howl of the grief from the villagers did not abate. But through the tumult, that first lesson came back to everyone. Old William, then others, began to repeat the words. "I believe. I believe. I believe." Over and over. And, powered by belief, the broken staff was made whole again.

The atmosphere began to lighten in waves. The wind slowly stilled. The air became as quiet as a midnight snow. Time itself seemed to stop. The villagers could feel magic all around them. And when they opened their eyes, there stood Ombric, looking so very Ombric-like! As if nothing had happened at all. And behind him stood the bear! His wounds were gone—vanished!—but his fur was now as white as a cloud. And in his giant front paws he held the man like a sleeping child.

Ombric took the staff that Katherine, beaming brighter than even the sunlight, held up to him. "Thank you for remembering," Ombric said. He ran his hands along the worn wood pensively, rubbing a thumb along the scar of the crack. Then he motioned to the man in the bear's arms. "The wounded stranger helped save us. It would be rude to not return the favor."

With a wave of his hand, Ombric started walking toward Big Root. In front of everyone's eyes, the tree began to revive. With Ombric's every step, new leaves budded forth and grew. With Ombric's every step, the shattered hearts of the villagers grew stronger. Magic had indeed returned to Santoff Claussen. And all of it would be needed to heal the young stranger who had saved their day.

CHAPTER ELEVEN

In Which Wisdom Is Proven to Be a Tricky Customer Indeed

DAYS PASSED AS NORTH drifted in and out of consciousness in Big Root. *Am I actually inside a tree? Is it the very same tree I'd seen fighting the bear? A tree that fought a bear?* North wasn't one to believe in magic. He believed only in his cunning mind and sureness with a blade. And yet ...

He had allowed himself to follow a crazy dream of treasure. He had ridden over water and clouds—on a twelve-hundred-pound horse!—and had turned his back on the riches that had doomed his men. These acts defied explanation. And now here he was, in a bed that seemed to understand his every thought or need. When he was uncomfortable, it adjusted and propped him up. When his bandaged legs ached, the bed gently kneaded at them until they felt better.

Food and drink hovered in the air beside him, though he was still too weak to even reach for them. But there was always a steady parade of three or four curious children, always bickering with one another over who got to spread jam on his toast, who got to hold a mug of hot broth or a cooling honey water to his lips, and—what seemed to cause the most heated arguments—who got to feed his horse. But the more North rested, the more his mind wondered and marveled at the many impossible things that had occurred.

The most impossible was that the wizard, the one he'd seen the bear devour, had survived. *How can this be?* His name, North learned, was Ombric, and he was alive and whole. He was applying elixirs and ointments and fussing over North as often as those children did. What a yammering bunch they were. Some days—the bad days, the days when the aches of wounds healing brought on fevers—their conversation seemed insane. Messages from insects, creatures called Fearlings, and a man in the Moon.

But slowly, North started to piece together the snatches of bizarre conversations. Then, one morning, he woke to find a little girl, the one who seemed to sit most often by his bedside, slipping a tiny, hand-sewn book of pictures next to his pillow. He feigned sleep until she left the room, then he lifted the small volume and sifted through the pages. They were filled with charcoal drawings of shadowy creatures and the black bear . . . and himself, guarding the children as if they were the tsar of Russia's treasures. There were sketches of a baby in a ship that sailed the heavens, of a battle on the Moon, and of a great villain who brought darkness and doom.

The tale was swirling in his head, colliding with what he remembered from that early morning duel, and filling in the gaps of what he'd once thought impossible and now believed was true. Had he really stopped that bear? The children assured him he had! The children explained that a demon named Pitch the Nightmare King had come for them, to take away their dreams. His minions, the Fearlings, hadn't been able to sneak into Santoff Claussen; the moonbeams were too effective at stopping them during the night. That Ombric fellow had figured out that Pitch couldn't attack during the day—since his defeat centuries ago, neither he nor his Fearlings could tolerate the light of the Moon or the sun. So Pitch had possessed the village's bear, forced him to do whatever he commanded. It seemed a perfect choice—being inside the bear was an ideal shield against light and was powerful enough to fight Ombric. Best of all, he would be trusted by the villagers. He was their friend.

To North it all still sounded like madness. Nightmare Kings? Enchanted forests? Then North thought more about the dream that had brought him to Santoff Claussen in the first place. It made him wonder. How could a dream show him a place he'd never seen? One day he felt strong enough to ask Ombric. The wizard's left eyebrow rose and he tried to suppress a smile. The children had noticed that Ombric had been *almost* smiling a great deal as the wounded bandit's condition improved.

"I asked the Man in the Moon for help," Ombric explained, lifting off then replacing a bandage on North's shin. "He gave you the dream. He thought you could be of assistance."

It was North's turn to raise his eyebrows. "Me?" He laughed out loud. "I'm better known for assisting gold pieces from a potentate's pocket than assisting Moon men, wizards, and little brats."

Ombric pursed his lips in amusement. "Perhaps he thought the King of the Bandits would be a worthy foe for the Nightmare King."

Well, North thought, *that's an answer worth considering.* "King of the Bandits" had a pleasing ring to it.

Then Ombric added, "But I suspect it was more than that."

North was puzzled by the remark. "And what in all these crazy worlds could that be? I'm a thief."

Ombric rubbed at the jagged crack in his staff. "Face the facts, my young friend. The forest that surrounds our village can clear a path only for the good of heart. You alone rejected the gold the Spirit of the Forest offered you. That never would have happened with a *real* bandit."

Not a real bandit? North thought angrily. *Why, I am the greatest thief alive! Perhaps in all of history!* But these thoughts felt, suddenly, hollow and somehow false. What was happening to him?

"You, or this place, or that Spirit have bewitched me!" he bellowed. "I am Nicholas St. North, the Bandit King! Nothing more or less!"

"No wizard or spirit has the power to change the human heart," Ombric replied with great calm.

"Liar!" shouted North.

Over the angry exchange, the tiny voice of

Katherine broke through. "But you were also our hero." She looked at him with more strength and purpose than he thought any child was capable of. "We were so afraid. And then you came."

North looked at Katherine and the other children who'd come closer as his anger had flared. There was something in their faces that he was barely beginning to fathom. Something he had never seen before: kindness. And though he fought it, he was soothed. His pain eased. Not just the pain of battle wounds, but the wounds he'd always ignored—the deep, lonely hurt of a loveless life.

North was quiet. Days went by without his saying a single word. The other children came and went, but Katherine always stayed. He learned she was a foundling. Her parents were trying to get to Santoff Claussen and they had become lost in a terrible blizzard outside the forest rim. They'd perished in the cold, but Katherine, just a toddler then, had stumbled to the edge of the forest. The trees took pity on her and, with their roots, lifted her up, passing her from tree to tree and vine to vine. The animals had joined in, first a band of squirrels and chipmunks, then the reindeer, and finally, the bear himself, who brought her to Ombric's front door. From that night on, she had lived in Big Root.

Her steady kindness to North was his greatest comfort and worst torment. He saw himself in her. He knew what it was like to be lost. And this haunted him.

As he continued to heal, he seemed to withdraw even further. North saw within the child's serious gray eyes a need, a hope, a wish that he'd fought since he could remember.

To have a friend.

His life had been so hard and ruthless. Friendship meant trusting someone, and that was a luxury he had never enjoyed. But he slowly began to soften. What danger could this little girl possibly pose? She wasn't a Cossack or a thief. She was just a lonely little girl.

One morning, after Katherine had cleared a mug of elderberry soup that he had not touched, North finally spoke.

"Thank you, Katherine," he said, his voice a little raspy from being quiet so long.

Katherine looked at him with that clear-eyed gaze that seemed to see right through him. "Just rest, Mr. North," she told him, a hint of a smile curling onto her lips as she resumed her post at the foot of his bed. They didn't need to say another word.

Friends don't need to.

CHAPTER TWELVE

Another Short but Intriguing Episode

WHILE NORTH RECOVERED IN Big Root, the spectral boy rollicked across the planet as he pleased, from the wilds of Canada to the Himalayas to Arabian desert sands, riding on the wind or on fleets of clouds he'd commandeer at his whim. He could outrun any moonbeam and took prankish pleasure in hiding from them. He could never sit still for long. It was as if he'd been locked inside for ten thousand rainy days. Which wasn't far from the truth. Being locked inside Pitch's cold heart had been like a prison. Still, it wasn't the dagger that kept Pitch paralyzed all that time, but the goodness of the spectral boy.

The boy thawed the tiny fragment of goodness that still lived inside Pitch and kept his evil frozen, unable to act.

A little bit of goodness can be very powerful against evil. But the boy needed light and warmth and life. He could not bear the burden of stunting Pitch forever. His glow would eventually weaken and die, and Pitch would have walked again. But now the spectral boy was free. He wanted, needed, to just *go*. To *see* whatever seized his attention.

This Earth was new to him, and he looked upon it in very simple terms. Things were either good or bad. Riding clouds was good. Fearlings and Nightmare Men were bad. He thought of people almost as simply. There were Small Ones (children)—they were good. And fun! They were playful and wild, like himself. As for the Tall Ones (grown-ups), his feelings were more complicated. Some were good and some were definitely bad.

And Pitch was worse than bad. Pitch meant to harm all Small Ones, especially those in Santoff Claussen. The boy wasn't exactly sure why Pitch wanted to hurt them, but he was sure that it wasn't fair. Or right. He thought it might be that they were so strong and happy that they never had nightmares. So no matter where he was or what far-flung corner of the planet he was exploring, come night, he would rush back to the village and hide near Big Root, watching and waiting.

He noticed that the Tall One named North had stayed in the village. He liked North a great deal. He was brave and strong and always kind to the Small Ones.

But there was something else about North that intrigued him. The old man named Ombric was teaching him how to do all sorts of fascinating things. Magical things. The boy had once peered into the window of Big Root and saw North intently reading a thick book by the fireplace. Ombric was going over ledgers at a table nearby. Sleeping in her own little bed was the girl they called Katherine. He liked her too— she was very brave for a Small One.

The spectral boy had the oddest sensation ... a memory of something familiar,

The spectral boy

something good. He didn't know the word for it, but what he felt was "friendship."

Then the moonbeams arrived and caught his attention. They were ready for their game of chase.

The clouds were waiting.

It was time to play.

But if Pitch or any of his kind returned to hurt these people, the boy would do his best to help them.

CHAPTER THIRTEEN

The Warrior Apprentice Proves to Be Clever

UNLIKE THE SPECTRAL BOY, Nicholas St. North only *thought* he knew what it was like to be cooped up too long. Before a week was up—his bruises hadn't even turned all the way from blue-black to yellow-green—he was back on his feet and doing a hundred pull-ups at a time on a sturdy birch branch. He had the strength and determination of a herd of mustangs. North hadn't touched a saber since the battle with the bear, for the slightest thought of a weapon sent dark, troubling images bubbling up to his brain: children cowering, claws raging, so much panic and screaming. Ombric had created Santoff Claussen as a sanctuary, and right now that was exactly what North needed. And so he took sanctuary in Ombric's books. To steal treasures from every country in Europe and the Russias, a bandit needed to read and speak in their various languages. So North had no trouble diving into ancient Italian texts or even Greek or Latin.

What was remarkable was North's consuming fascination with spells and histories. And that Ombric even allowed the young man to study his books of magic. Their secrets were too powerful and could only be shared with those who Ombric thought would not be corrupted by their knowledge. Something about North interested the old wizard. He saw in him potential.

Santoff Claussen had always been a charmed

place, literally. For much longer than anyone could remember, Ombric had used all his powers and abilities to protect it from real evil. No thief, savage, or ruffian had ever successfully trespassed its defenses. Pitch, with his dark ways, was the first genuine wickedness the village had had to face.

The experience had affected everyone—grownups, children, even the forest and its creatures. They went about their lives as they had before, but the freewheeling joys of the past came less easily now. The trees in the enchanted forest were ever watchful. The animals were skittish as they worried about every shadow. Even the Spirit of the Forest felt anxious. "I have no power to use against Pitch," she sighed. "My treasures are not to his liking."

The children were not sleeping well. Ombric felt at fault. "I was too precious with this place," he confided to North. "Kept too much of the harshness of life from making its way in."

But the idea actually amused the wounded North. "You did fine, old man!" he reassured him, laughing. And though the children's parents were so distracted that virtually all inventing in the village had stopped, it was not so with North.

North was growing more and more enchanted with the village—and with the idea of "enchantment." Spells, legerdemain, conjuring—all came quite naturally to him, and it did not take long for the villagers (and Ombric himself) to consider him the wizard's first and only apprentice. North quickly became masterful in the alchemical arts, making Big Root bustle with activity again—or with the explosion of a spell that didn't go quite right. He worked with gusto, and regularly overstepped his new abilities without properly thinking things through. When creating a ball that would never stop bouncing, he added too much bounce. After the ball hit the ground, it rocketed up to the sky with such force that it could easily have traveled to Mars.

In another experiment he tried to make a young cat stay forever kitten-size. First, he accidentally shrunk the animal to the size of a microbe, then overcompensated. A regular-sized kitten is cute, but one that is twelve feet tall is a problem. The cat tried to eat Petrov and the bear repeatedly, even after being returned to a normal size.

This was all a welcome diversion for the village, a chance to laugh again. But North was not the type to take setbacks in stride. He fumed for days whenever things didn't go as he'd intended. Sometimes these angry moods would cause small catastrophes.

Furniture would burst into flames, or very small thunderclouds (usually no bigger than a pillow) would follow North around until he calmed.

"Knowledge without wisdom," Ombric remarked sagely, watching the kitten leap after Petrov's tail, causing the horse to knock over a wagon, "can get a bit messy."

North knew the wizard wasn't trying to provoke him, but regardless, it felt like a challenge. No longer able to settle hard feelings with a duel or a round of arm wrestling, he instead went back to work, determined not to fail.

Ombric admired his student's willingness to keep at it, despite the lad's outbursts of temper. But, just like he'd been as an outlaw, North was also extravagantly cheerful and charming and always ready with a story, especially for the children. If Ombric imparted knowledge and wonder to them, North was now their guide to adventure and good times. In fact, he was no longer a thief of treasures but a buccaneer of fun. He regaled them with tall tales of his early life. He claimed to know of a kingdom governed by a giant egg that ruled from its perch atop an ancient wall. He'd seen a cow that could jump higher than the Earth's atmosphere. North's stories were as soothing a tonic to the battle-scarred children as anything Ombric could have concocted from a medicine bottle. And little Katherine was the most rapt of all, devouring his stories and scribbling versions of them in her journals. It was apparent that the children adored North and, subsequently, so did their parents.

As North continued on as the wizard's apprentice, he became interested in ways to combine Ombric's old magic with the curious mechanical devices that the villagers loved to build. It could be claimed that the birth of what we now call "machines" began in Santoff Claussen. There were mechanical brooms that could sweep indefinitely. Small boxes that could fit over both ears and play music of one's choosing. Special magnifying glasses that, when pointed at the sun, could focus the rays and actually cook food. North eyed those inventions with the glint of thievery in his eyes.

"I'd have stolen all the wealth in Asia, Europe, and Africa, too, with any one of those toys," he told Ombric one morning at breakfast. The wizard looked at him quizzically. Katherine frowned. "Don't worry, either of you. Those pastimes are behind me now. I've plans to make my own device—something truly new."

Katherine was delighted. "I know you'll do something grand." Her confidence in him quieted his boastfulness. He did, after all, want to please her. Ombric, however, felt a pang of unease. He knew that North liked to tease him. Yet he sometimes worried, *Have I made the right choice?* But one thing was certain: Nicholas St. North had brilliant imaginative instincts. With luck and guidance, the lad could achieve great things. Things that Ombric could probably never imagine.

"Well, old boy, get ready for something you've never seen. I'm ready to combine man-made devices with your ancient hocus-pocus," North proclaimed, levitating honey into Ombric's cup. The wizard regarded his apprentice carefully. He knew he was getting old, and his alchemy would need youth, newness, chance, and a change to stay magical. But there were some risks.

"Mix the old and new with great caution. Remember, Nicholas, there can be dangers in the unknown."

North nodded, receptive to the advice, but eager to begin. He had a fantastic idea. An idea that would change all their lives! And while he'd grown very fond of the old man, he found his caution amusing. *He's been talking to bugs and reading books too long,* he thought. *Those bouncing balls and the giant kitten weren't so dangerous. And my new idea would pose no such risk.*

North knew exactly what his first experiment would be. He would make a mechanical man of magic—a robot djinni that would do wonders, but only when commanded. Cook for them! Clean! Help the children with their studies (which, North felt, they spent far too much time doing). What could possibly go wrong with that?

As for Ombric, he'd keep a watchful eye on his apprentice, but in truth, he was glad to have North distracted and even more glad at how North occupied the children. For Ombric had important work to do—the most important work of his long life: He must find a way to stop Pitch. He knew full well that they had not defeated the Nightmare King completely. They had only checked him, like players in a game of chess. And the old wizard knew that the game was far from over.

CHAPTER FOURTEEN

Wherein Wizard and Apprentice Make Discoveries That Prove to Be Momentous

MAKING A MECHANICAL MAN is not an easy task for any wizard, and North was still very much a student. But the construction of his robot djinni had caught the interest of the entire village and further steadied the mood of Santoff Claussen. Plans had to be drawn. Methods and materials were discussed, argued over, agreed upon.

They toiled away in the workroom in Big Root. North consulted ancient scrolls and dusty texts he'd found in the darkest corner of Ombric's cupboard and then discussed with the villagers the proper tensions of a pulley that would serve as an elbow or knee of the djinni.

"The djinni has to know us—like a good horse knows its rider!" North decided. He based his theory on an old trick for domesticated Siberian tigers, who slept in nests of their masters' clothes as a safeguard against rebellion. "Get me your lucky penny, your favorite rock, your mother's comb. I'll put them in the djinni's chest."

The children were in charge of assembling the precious trove. There were many debates over whether a shoe was more personal than a locket, a pocketknife more cherished than a beloved pebble. After days of gathering valuables together, the children rushed to the workroom, treasures in hand. North carefully placed each item in a small hinged box. He was just about to tuck it into the cavity by the djinni's heart when Katherine dashed up, waving a scrap of paper—a drawing of North himself.

"Will the djinni know us both from this?" she asked. North looked from the childish drawing to the small girl in front of him. He looked to the drawing again—at the detailing Katherine had added. He looked grand, noble, heroic even. Was that how she saw him? He unhinged the box and gently laid the paper on top of the other items, but in truth, he most wanted to fold it into his pocket, to keep it for his own.

He realized with a start that Katherine, in her quiet way, was waiting for a reply. "Indeed it will," he assured her. "It'll recognize the portrait, and know whose hand has made it." At that, the children huddled close as he sealed the box and carefully placed it inside the djinni's chest.

"Is it finished?" asked Fog.

"Soon enough," North told him. He looked down proudly at his mechanical creation. At nearly eight feet tall, it was shaped like a man but built entirely of metal gears and clockwork, all in shades of metal—silver, bronze, copper, gold, and darker tones like gunmetal and iron. It was strangely beautiful, like something that hadn't been made but had been dreamed into being. Around the chest, shoulders, and joints were plates that resembled armor but with intricate, graceful curves. The face and head were simply shaped, yet had a handsomeness that recalled a finely made toy. One slim silver key protruded from the area over the heart—that's how North intended to wind up the djinni, he'd explained to the children.

All told, there was a wondrous quality about it that surprised them all, especially North. He'd built weapons and shields before. But the robot djinni was designed to do only good, and it looked the part.

North fastened the last chest plate over the treasure box, then turned the silver key five, six, seven times. There was a soft, almost musical whir of sound, then the robot djinni sat up. It looked at them with a curious expression, not of surprise, but as if it had been *expecting* to see them, and appeared to smile. North and the children erupted in cheers.

"What is your command?" the djinni asked in a smooth, measured voice.

They were all caught off guard. A first command! They hadn't thought of what their first command would be! Then North spoke up. "Katherine, you may give the order."

Katherine's eyes widened, a rosy glow creeping onto her cheeks. She thought for a moment, then in her most polite voice said, "I should like you, Djinni, to walk outside, please." The djinni nodded just as politely and did as she asked.

The group followed the djinni out the door of Big Root and into the light of day. And Nicholas St. North, for the first time in his wild, adventurous life, felt that he had done something truly fine.

Ombric, however, was unaware of his pupil's success. He was locked inside his own room, lost in his studies. He had made considerable progress: With the use of a millennium's worth of astrological records,

The robot djinni

along with charts yellowed with age, and bits of stories and legends, he was able to piece together a plan he hoped would stop Pitch.

He'd discovered that five relics of the *Moon Clipper* had fallen to Earth, scattered across the globe after the great explosion. But, Ombric reasoned, if they were *brought together*, they could hold great power—a far greater power than that of the wisps of ancient stardust that had enriched the ground of Santoff Claussen, and perhaps even greater power than that of the moonbeams.

Ombric had been tracing the location of the five pieces. *We must gather the closest first*, he murmured, rolling a chart back up and tying it with a thin leather cord. But he alone knew that getting to the first stop would be the most dangerous journey of his very long life.

CHAPTER FIFTEEN

Partly Cloudy and Most Unfair

THE DJINNI HAD BECOME the undisputed center of excitement in the village. It was able to do almost any task it was asked. "Djinni, can you move these boulders?" asked one of Old William's sons, Not-as-Old William. "I was thinking of making a new tower."

"As you command," replied the mechanical man, and in minutes it had assembled, quite artfully, the hulking stones into a splendid tower, complete with turrets.

Other villagers made requests of the djinni, but one day Katherine had a request she desperately wanted to make and North could read her impatience. "Djinni! The lass will explode if she doesn't get her turn next," he boomed. Katherine bounced on her toes in anticipation—she had been drawing pictures of the jumping cow North had told them about and wondered what it had seen when it had leaped in the sky.

The djinni turned to her, and she asked excitedly, "Djinni, can you throw me as high into the air as you can and catch me?"

"As you command," it answered. And quite effortlessly, it tossed Katherine so high that the villagers lost sight of her. They peered into the sky worriedly, North using a telescope of his own design.

"There she is!" he said at last, pointing to the small bank of clouds Katherine was gleefully skimming over.

Though the others watched uneasily, Katherine was delighted by her sudden journey into the atmosphere. She'd soared above the tallest trees in Santoff Claussen and passed a flock of startled geese. She soared higher than she had even imagined; below her, Santoff Claussen looked rather small, and the outside world very large and inviting. She trusted the djinni to catch her—after all, North had made it.

Then, floating just a few feet in front of her, was a small cloud, not much bigger than a feather bed. On that cloud, to her complete and utter surprise, crouched . . . a boy. The same boy who had come to their rescue back in the forest! He was looking right at her. Katherine gasped—she had seen him only that one time. In daylight he shimmered even more brilliantly. He looked as if he were made of light and mist, like a breath on a cold winter's night, and . . .

and . . . how was it that he could stand on a cloud? She stared, stunned.

They had only a single second together. She smiled at him. He smiled back. She reached out her hand, and he did as well. Their fingertips were just about to touch. Then she began to drop.

Whereas going up had been a delicious mix of terror and glee for Katherine, falling the rest of the way back down was entirely different. She was so deep in thought about the strange enchanted boy that she was barely aware that she was hurtling toward Earth. Nor did she notice Ombric emerge from Big Root, lean on his staff, and watch. She landed—to North's great relief—gently and comfortably in the djinni's outstretched arms. A wisp of wind touched her cheek, and she glanced up toward the small cloud once more.

"I knew it'd catch her. I built it that way," North blustered as everyone cheered. But that didn't stop his heart from pounding until the djinni tipped Katherine firmly onto the grass.

"What if it'd missed her?" cried William the Almost Youngest, sounding a bit disappointed that things had gone so smoothly.

"Djinni, I want to be able to become invisible!" demanded William the Absolute Youngest.

Sunlight glinted off the djinni's shoulders. It paused, then, giving a sweeping bow, said, "That is a wish I cannot grant."

"But why not? You're supposed to do anything we ask!" said William the Almost Youngest.

"I am a djinni of the possible. I can do anything a machine or mortal may, but more effectively. To make you invisible would take magic. And magic is only for those with the wisdom to wield its power." Then it bowed again humbly.

Ombric gave a cough and strode up to the djinni, peering at every inch of it. He did not say a word. The villagers held their breath, half expecting Ombric to be displeased, though they weren't sure why. And North knew to bite his tongue entirely. *Tough old bird,* he thought. *I'm sure he'll find fault.*

But to North's surprise, Ombric tapped at the djinni's chest, traced a finger over the silver key, and pronounced, "Admirable piece of work. Well built and wisely conceived. It will be of great use for our journey." He turned to North and stamped his staff on the ground. "Nicholas, pack your things and ready your djinni! We leave on a mission of greatest importance at dawn."

Katherine glanced up. "Am I to come too?"

The old wizard's face softened. "No, my girl." He took her hand. "You must stay here. I expect you to help the bear and Petrov protect the village while we are gone."

Katherine swallowed hard and agreed, but she was deeply disappointed. If adventures were to be had, she wanted to see them and drew them in her sketchbook. North felt disappointed for Katherine as well—there was nothing like an adventure to make the blood race and the cheeks flush. The djinni, of course, could feel nothing—it was just a machine.

But that would all change soon enough—and Katherine would have an adventure to match any in her young life.

CHAPTER SIXTEEN

Anger, Age, and Fear Make an Unwanted Appearance

THE REST OF THE day was wild with activity and confusion: Things were packed and reconsidered and packed again. No one in the village could recall an instance when Ombric had ventured on a journey away from Santoff Claussen, so this was an occasion of considerable conjecture. North, having been a warrior, understood the need for secrecy—before he'd come to Santoff Claussen, he'd only truly ever trusted Petrov fully. So although Ombric hadn't told North, or anyone, where they were going, he headed straight to work. With the djinni's help, he crafted a new set of swords and daggers forged from bits of the ancient meteor that had marked the founding of the village. "Rich with stardust," North remarked to the djinni. "The old man claims they can ward off any shadow."

"So let it be done," replied the djinni with a bow. The mechanical man's response bemused North.

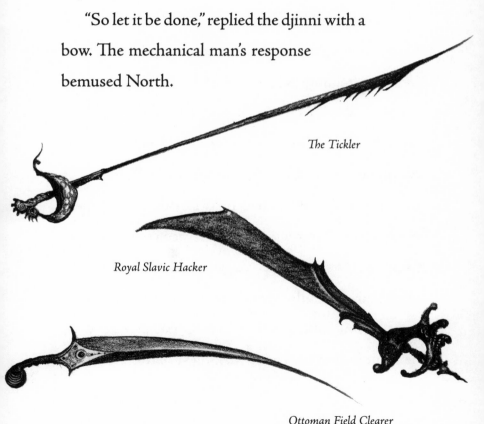

The Tickler

Royal Slavic Hacker

Ottoman Field Clearer

North stood in the middle of Big Root, sharpening the new swords. "One must be more cunning than the enemy," he remarked thoughtfully to Ombric, who had wandered over to see how he was coming along. "And Pitch is as crafty as they come."

The old man nodded and replied, "Clever lad."

And though wild Cossack horses couldn't get him to admit it aloud, North basked in the old man's rare compliment.

By nightfall the packing was done, the preparations made, and Katherine had insisted on helping them every step of the way, but she'd been quieter than usual. In fact, Ombric realized, she'd barely said a word since he'd informed everyone that he and North were leaving. She was overtired, Ombric decided, so he conjured up her room, making sure to thicken the oval of moss that served as her carpet and adding an extra drop of richness to her hot chocolate.

But that wasn't at all what Katherine wanted. What she wanted—desperately—was to go with them. "I'm big enough!" she insisted. "I could help!"

"What do you think, Apprentice?" Ombric asked North as he lit her candles. "Should she journey with us? Or stay, as I suggest?"

North considered long and hard before he answered. Katherine grew hopeful that North would side with her. He must. He was her champion! But though he hated to say it, North knew the wizard was right. "It's too dangerous, Katherine. Your place is here. It's best for you and for us."

To Katherine, these words seemed a total betrayal. So when North wished her good night, she refused to respond. He said good night a second time, and she turned her face to the wall in stony silence.

North understood—he, too, had never been one to take no for an answer. But her silence hurt him. *I can outfight anything that breathes, and yet this child wounds me worse than any bullet or blade,* he thought, and steeled his resolve to keep her at home, safe. Still, as he left her room, he waved his right hand with an angry jerk that caused all the candles in the room to extinguish—a spell he had just learned and, in his anger, perfected. He tromped up the stairs to the lab and slammed the door.

Ombric hovered by Katherine's bed, frowning in the dark. "The boy is brave but unruly," he muttered. "He may never make a proper wizard." No sooner had he said this than he heard a cough come from the lab, and with a soft hiss, a single candle on Katherine's night table relit itself. A dim but warm glow returned to the room.

Just as quickly, Katherine leaned over and resentfully blew out the candle. She flopped back down and pulled the sheets over her head.

Ombric shook his head in bemusement. All this drama and anger. Well, that was what youth was like, he remembered. Calm comes with age. And Ombric had been feeling very old of late. The fight with Pitch and the bear had left him weary and uneasy; his confidence shaken. Was he powerful enough to stand up to Pitch again? Would Nicholas be ready to take over if the worst were to happen? North had not been tested as a wizard yet, and this, too, worried Ombric. But he knew he must stay the course now. Stay focused and steady. Pitch counted on fear. Used it as a weapon. And Ombric could not let it get the best of him.

He summoned a glowworm to provide a spot of light in Katherine's room, then headed for the lab himself, the climb never having felt so exhausting. But he was pleased to see that North was in the process of double-checking their gear for the trip. They were bringing a vast array of instruments, books, elixirs, potions, and weapons, but everything fit in a smallish backpack. He called it his "infinity bag"—he designed it to hold whatever anyone put into it. "I once packed an entire mountain and castle in it," he'd explained when North had looked at the satchel skeptically.

It did, however, weigh as much as whatever it contained. "A problem I've never been able to solve," Ombric admitted. "But that's why your djinni will come in most handy. I assume it can handle the load?"

"And then some," North assured him. The djinni bowed in agreement.

"Then we must rest, for we leave at first light," said the wizard, and he climbed into the highly unusual assemblage that constituted his bed. North had been dumbfounded when he'd first seen it—a giant globe that swung open into sections as Ombric neared. The inside was hollow except for a wooden rod near its bottom, which Ombric stood on. The globe was surrounded by a dozen or so owls on perches with their wings tucked at their sides, their eyes shut. Ombric assumed a stance that very closely mimicked theirs, and closed his eyes as well. The globe then folded shut, each owl letting out a quiet hoot as it did. Ombric was now settled in for the night.

Nicholas St. North had slept in many odd places—in trees, on the edges of cliffs, under the bed of a sleeping maharaja—but those times were about making do. Ombric clearly preferred this bed; it was his home. Wizards were an odd bunch, it seemed to North.

But that's not what he pondered that night. Nor did his mind spin with worries of the upcoming journey and what they might face. Instead he thought over and over about Katherine, and how she was still angry with him. He forced himself to think of something else.

He wondered if the djinni actually slept. North softly treaded to the workroom and peered in. Ombric's globe, high above, sighed with gentle snores. The djinni was upright, but seemed to be resting.

"Good night, Djinni," North whispered.

"As you command" came the reply.

North hadn't intended it as an order, so the response amused him. When he returned to bed, he began to imagine other things that one could say that the djinni would misinterpret. If North mentioned to the djinni in passing to "have a good day," would the djinni try to make a rainy day sunny? Soon he was distracted from Katherine's anger and at last fell asleep. . . . But the djinni did not.

A small black spider was lowering itself down on a single strand of silk toward the djinni's left ear. Spiders were quite common in Big Root; Ombric spoke to them often. But this spider was different. It scampered delicately into the djinni's ear.

Pitch was indeed as clever as they come.

CHAPTER SEVENTEEN
A Twist and Turn

WHEN KATHERINE AWOKE THE next morning, Big Root was quiet. Too quiet. There was none of the jolly clatter that accompanied the beginning of their days. She did not hear North's wild laughter as he tried out new spells or Ombric's distracted humming.

They left without saying good-bye! she realized, her heart sinking. There was, however, a full breakfast hovering next to her bed and, with it, a small box with a note. She reached for the mug of warm cocoa and took a sip. It was Ombric's brew. He made it with less chocolate than North, who always put in just a little more than necessary. She was never sure whose she liked best; they were both good in their own way. Then she turned to the box. She suspected it was North's doing—Ombric would have at least wrapped it in muslim. As she slowly opened it, she thought, *This is their way of telling me they will miss me.* Wizards, she was learning, were more about deeds than words.

Inside the box was a round device. It was gold and weighty, like a clock. But it had only one hand and no numbers; on the tip of the hand was the single letter *N*. She unfolded the note that lay underneath. It read:

> *Dear Katherine,*
> *If there is trouble, you can always find me.*
> *The arrow will point the way.*
> *Yours,*

Her unhappiness dissipated a fraction. It was so like North. Only he would make a compass that pointed to himself.

Katherine also knew it was his way of testing her. She could leave and follow them if she wanted. But they had asked her to stay with Petrov and the bear to keep an eye on things, and so she would. Still, she couldn't help but wish there would be a smidgeon of trouble, so she would have an excuse to go after them. The thought made her grin. But Ombric always said, "Be careful what you wish for." She finished her cocoa and decided that wizards were annoying. Still, she threaded the compass's chain through her buttonhole and admired it once more.

Katherine went about her day as she'd promised, freshening Petrov's hay and keeping the bear company, her new compass dangling against her blouse.

She vowed not to look at it, but every hour or so she glanced down, keeping an eye on which way it pointed. North and Ombric were moving quickly southeast, she could tell, and it couldn't have been much past dawn when they'd snuck off.

North and Ombric had indeed left at dawn. It had been a massive undertaking, with lots of equipment and contraptions packed into the infinity bag that complicated the journey. Ombric had to admit that North's ingenious djinni was a major breakthrough in the blending of ancient magic and the magic of man. As they'd prepared to leave, Ombric had lamented how, even with the djinni carrying all of their supplies, it would be a slow and exhausting trek. But North had had a surprise for the old wizard.

"Djinni, take us up!" he'd commanded in a voice

too chipper for that early in the morning. The djinni bowed as usual, but suddenly from its back, shoulders, and arms there began to emerge the most beautiful and elaborate flying sleigh! Its every floorboard, deck, and bolt was a mechanical extension of the djinni itself.

With their gear finally aboard, North turned to his teacher, trying not to look overly pleased with himself.

"We are ready, I suppose?" asked Ombric slyly, but he didn't wait for an answer. He climbed aboard, sat in what was obviously the captain's chair, and proceeded to examine the controls. North attempted to explain how the flying machine worked, but Ombric interrupted: "Doubly clever you are, Nicholas, but I have studied Master da Vinci too."

The old man recognized that North had taken

much of the craft's design from the famous Leonardo da Vinci's sketchbooks, which were in the Big Root library as part of Ombric's conjured collection.

"Da Vinci and I were good friends, you know," the wizard continued. "However, his design never worked properly."

North shrugged. "I've made some improvements." He pulled a lever, touched a button, then twisted a key. The propellers began to spin, and within seconds, the "flyer" took to the sky.

By evening they were more than a thousand miles away from Santoff Claussen. Every now and then Ombric glanced at his pocket globe and determined where they should turn next.

"Head twenty degrees to the west!" he shouted above the wind, and the djinni, of course, piloted them as ordered. Ombric still hadn't shared the secret of their destination, but North had a pretty good idea of where they were. In fact, their destination filled the sky in front of them. It was impossible to miss.

"The Himalayas!" The tallest mountains in the world—vast, snow-covered, beautiful, and forbidding. North had never seen them—there'd never been anything there he'd wanted to steal. Thievery was not on his mind at the moment, though. Just excitement and anticipation. *What's the old boy got us into?* he wondered. Would there be a battle? North hadn't been in combat for months. He hadn't tangled with so much as a stubborn jar lid since Pitch had attacked Big Root. Still, he felt certain that by adding his new knowledge of magic and spells to his arsenal of weaponry, he'd be more formidable than ever. Plus, the djinni was armed—North had given it one of his best swords. What a warrior it'd make!

Travel by djinni is more comfortable than one would think.

With the strength of a hundred men and the obe-
dience of a trained wolfhound, nothing short of an
avalanche could stop his invention!

While North reveled in confidence, Katherine was
mired in boredom. It had been a long, listless day back
in Santoff Claussen. She'd ridden the outer perimeter
of the village over a dozen times, hoping for some
small trouble or adventure, but apparently, all was
well. Petrov was equally restless, and he savored any
chance to ride with Katherine. And ride they did. A
horse was so much easier to handle than a reindeer;
plus, there was a saddle! Katherine loved to ride hard
and fast just for the thrill of it. The bear had come by
several times to assure Katherine that the forest was
calm, quiet, functioning as usual. Some of the fur on
his chin was turning back to black, which made him

The bear

appear to have a rather dashing goatee. It reminded Katherine of North.

The only event of consequence that day was also the worst: Petrov had tripped as they rode back to Big Root for the evening. His left hoof had gotten caught by the uneven gash where Pitch had melted back into the earth all those weeks ago. Everyone in the village avoided the spot except for Katherine and Petrov, who took a certain pleasure in galloping over it, stomping it down further each time.

Fortunately, his leg wasn't broken, but he'd given it a good twist and was limping badly as Katherine walked him to his stable by Big Root. They wouldn't be riding again for at least a few days.

As she readied for bed that evening, Katherine had an unsettling feeling. Perhaps it was because of Petrov's accident, or maybe Big Root felt empty without Ombric and North. It felt worse than loneliness: It felt more like dread.

Katherine's last chore of the day was to feed Ombric's owls. She'd been so distracted by this uneasy feeling that she'd nearly forgotten about them. Dressed in her nightgown, holding a candle in one hand and the owls' favorite tidbits in the other, she made her way to Ombric's lab. When she opened the door, she stared in surprise. His library was uncharacteristically messy. They'd left in a hurry, to be sure, and North wasn't quite as fastidious as Ombric, but still, what a mess!

Thinking how pleased they'd both be to come back to a neat workplace, Katherine began to straighten things after she'd fed the owls. She could barely make heads or tails of the peculiar writings and drawings—they were in Latin or French or some ancient language she didn't yet know. She was surrounded by things that were at once familiar and yet strange and unknowable.

As Katherine was about to close one of the books, something caught her eye. There were several odd indentations in the soft, pulpy paper. Ombric took impeccable care of his books; he even wore gloves when he leafed through some of the most ancient of them. She'd never seen anything like these marks in his books before. She turned a dozen or so pages and found the same small dents. But they weren't dents at all—they were fingerprints!

She grabbed one of the many magnifying glasses that were scattered among the clutter. There seemed to be a pattern within each mark—swirls, as in real fingerprints, but more graceful and unusual. She'd seen something like it before, but where? As she struggled to connect her memories, the feeling of dread deepened, and when the pieces came together, she stopped in a panic. The robot djinni! These were *its* prints. She knew Ombric would never entrust these spells to a machine. While Ombric slept, the djinni must have been studying his books!

Katherine hurriedly looked at the book's cover. She could decipher the easy part. *Spells of . . .* Of what? Of what? She'd never seen the next word before and needed to consult two different dictionaries to piece it together, but once she did, she gasped. The title read *Spells of Enslavement.*

CHAPTER EIGHTEEN

Sly Is the Evil That Travels Unknown

I**T HAD BEEN ROUGHLY** an hour since Ombric had started to suspect that the djinni was now likely controlled by Pitch. A tiny detail had raised Ombric's suspicions, something that only an ancient wizard would notice. He was certain that North was unaware that something was amiss; North was agog at the sight of the Himalayas; he'd let his warrior guard down. But what the ever vigilant Ombric had noticed was that the djinni was admiring the mountains too. Subtly and furtively, as if it did not want to be noticed. And Ombric knew that this was something that no machine would do on its own.

A machine could not be curious. A machine could not feel interest or awe. It could only do as it was told, and neither Ombric nor North had ordered the djinni to do anything but fly them as instructed.

Ombric shut his eyes and concentrated.

Even from miles away, he could still communicate mentally with his owls in Big Root. Within a few seconds, he heard them. *Katherine gave us more food than you do*, they said. *We want bigger portions from now on*. It took some mental wrangling, but eventually, the drowsy, well-fed owls were able to focus on the questions the wizard was asking them.

One of them remembered having seen a spider just above the djinni's head the night before. The owl had thought nothing of it and had gone back to sleep—spiders in Big Root were not an unusual occurrence; they told marvelous jokes and were awfully good at tickling.

What sort of spider? Ombric inquired silently.

An odd spider, the owl responded. *Completely black. A wolf spider, I believe.*

That was all Ombric needed to know. Russian Wolf spiders were dormant in winter. He knew that much, and the likely conclusion was this: Pitch had made his way through Ombric's defenses in what at first glance was the most simple of guises—a house spider.

But how to proceed? With Pitch now controlling the djinni, Ombric knew that his and North's best chance was to catch the robot off guard and defeat it. But could they defeat a machine of that strength? A machine, Ombric recalled with a cringe, that was armed with one of North's hand-forged swords?

And it was more than their own safety at stake. Pitch was clearly out for them both, and he was probably after the lost relics of the *Moon Clipper* as well. *The djinni must not get near our true destination*, Ombric determined. There was no telling what Pitch would do if he found what they were looking for—and the power it surely possessed. And they were quickly honing in on that place now. . . . Ombric had to try to trick the djinni. He would need to rely on incantations and magic, and timing would be everything.

"The base of that peak—that's the place. Land there, Djinni!" Ombric shouted out quickly, pointing to the mountain looming ahead of them.

"As you command," said the djinni, and with a slight shift in direction, it guided the ship down to the snowy drifts below.

Ombric tried to catch North's attention, but the apprentice was too busy looking about the landscape. Cheeks flushed, whether with cold or excitement, Ombric could not tell, North asked, "Is this the spot?"

"Indeed it is, Nicholas," replied the wizard. "We'll find what we seek hidden under tons of rock and snow. But thanks to you, we have the djinni to dig it out."

North continued to gaze about intensely. "Perfect place for an ambush," he muttered. "We're sitting ducks for any force that might lie in wait." He drew both swords and stepped out of the sled, alert and ready.

Ombric knew he'd have to be very careful now. He gripped his staff tightly. A machine could be stopped by one spell. But if that machine was controlled by an evil from inside, it would be much more difficult.

Ombric's feet crunched the snow as he tried not to pace. He sifted through his memory, seeking the most effective incantations.

Then he had it. Two spells spoken simultaneously without hesitation or flaw could do the trick. Such an incantation would take four seconds, maybe five. But five seconds was a long time when faced with a situation this dangerous. Ombric would need to distract the djinni and time his spells with perfection.

"Djinni," Ombric began, "retract your airship and prepare to dig." What happened next was almost imperceptible, but Ombric saw it: The djinni hesitated. And now Ombric was certain. The djinni was possessed. As he was thinking this, the djinni began folding the ship back into itself.

Ombric had the spells clearly in his mind.

He was ready to blurt them out when suddenly,

without warning, North attacked the djinni!

Even more quickly, the robot unsheathed its own sword and deflected North's blows.

"I knew it! It's possessed, Ombric!" North cried out. "I didn't *tell* it to defend itself!" North slashed furiously at the djinni, but the robot met every one of North's thrusts.

A fleeting moment of pride in North's good intuition flashed through Ombric's mind, but he couldn't dwell on it, for now was the time! Invoking two spells at once is something only the greatest wizards can do, and Ombric was doing it flawlessly.

Equally flawlessly, North was fighting the djinni; his precision, fed by his fury, was uncanny. *I can't recall ever fighting better,* North was thinking, while Ombric was racing to utter the last of the spells.

Just as the wizard thought he was going to make

it—he found he suddenly had no control over his mouth. It felt . . . frozen. Then the icy feeling spread to his face, then shoulders, until his whole body was stiff and paralyzed, and it was shrinking, shrinking. He fell to the ground with a small thud. Followed by a second one. North. The two found themselves suddenly lying in the snow, unable to move. The djinni looked down at them both. A dark and terrible laugh echoed from deep inside its chest. It was a laugh like no other. It was the laugh of Pitch. "May I be your apprentice too, Master Ombric?" he snarled. "I learned your spells of enslavement quickly enough!"

North struggled to look over at Ombric, but he couldn't even blink. Then he began to realize that he wasn't just paralyzed.

"You're *my* slaves now!" gloated the djinni. "My little puppets."

It was true. They'd been turned into small porcelain versions of themselves, no bigger than dolls.

The djinni hunkered beside them, casting a massive shadow over their tiny bodies. "Now tell me of this weapon you seek."

CHAPTER NINETEEN

The Telltale Hoot

No sooner had Katherine made the alarming discovery concerning the djinni than every owl roosting in Ombric's lab began to hoot. They obviously had received a message from the wizard.

Katherine spoke very little owl (for all its seeming simplicity, owl was one of the most subtle and difficult bird languages to master), but she listened intently and managed to understand one key word.

"Danger!" she cried out, and the owls nodded in confirmation. She rushed to Ombric's globe. "Show me where!" she pleaded, turning back to the owls.

They pointed with their beaks to a vast white area in the central Himalayas.

"Ombric and North are in danger?" she asked one last time, as if wanting to be absolutely sure.

The owls seemed to understand for they hooted vigorously.

Katherine had waited a long time to have her own great adventure, and now the chance was here. It seemed she had the instincts for it. Perhaps this was something that had been passed down from her parents. As a foundling, she'd never know for sure. It took her only moments to formulate a plan.

The lead owl is always the first to answer.

She was surprised by how natural it seemed. Then she took action.

"Fly to the forest. Bring the reindeer," she commanded the owls, miming the order with her hands. The owls took off with a loud rustling of feathers. She looked at the compass North had given her. It pointed the way. She ran to her room. It would be cold and dangerous where she was going. She would need a coat and a dagger.

CHAPTER TWENTY

In Which a Twist of Fate Begets a Knot in the Plan

PITCH'S SCHEME HAD WORKED more beautifully than he had dared hope. He was supremely happy with the djinni's protective metal shell. Not only was he now safe from sun and moonlight, but he could move about as easily as he could in his own shadowy form. Granted, in the robot's body he could not turn to vapor or grow to the size of a thundercloud, but it reminded him of what it had been like to be an actual *being*— solid, substantial, *real*. Something no child or adult could dismiss as a mere nightmare or imagined vision.

In the months since he'd been freed from the cave, Pitch and his minions had found their way to almost every corner of the globe, leaving fear and unease in their wake. But there'd been limits to this new freedom that were frustrating him. At night he could be as fearsome as any creature that ever existed. He had learned to summon clouds to block the Moon's interfering light. In pure dark, he was pure evil, capable of flooding whomever he chose with torturous nightmares.

However, with the coming of every dawn, he and his henchmen had been forced into retreat. The light of day had the power to undo all his work! Adults dismissed their encounters with him as having never happened; they were just "bad dreams." And they convinced their children of the same.

Even worse, children had taken to calling him the

"Boogeyman," a name he despised. And though they feared him, they did not entirely believe in him, either. But now—now!—he would be something they could see at any hour. *Now* he was something they could not deny.

This, of course, was not enough. New knowledge and weapons would be needed to conquer the day. Plaguing children with nightmares was just the beginning, he now realized. To achieve his goal, those nightmares would have to be *believed*.

He felt more powerful than ever. No force could stop him. The bear, that meddlesome tree—they would all fall to him now, as quickly as that idiotic old wizard and his feckless apprentice had.

But first . . .

First there was the matter of the device, the weapon, the *thing* that the old wizard had set out to find. If the wizard believed this weapon could destroy *him*, then it must be very powerful indeed.

Pitch plucked up his two miniaturized captives and turned them this way and that, demanding answers. But he was not getting the ones he needed. Ombric would not or could not speak. No matter how many times Pitch ordered him to reveal what and where this "weapon" was, the toy-size wizard lay mute. And North could not answer for the simple reason that he did not know. Ombric had never told him where they were going or what they were hoping to find.

North was seething with anger. He was trapped by the very creature he had set out to destroy—and he had no one to blame but himself. Why hadn't he listened when Ombric had warned him of the danger that the merging of old and new magic could bring? North felt a deep and crushing shame—and a feeling that was wholly unfamiliar: helplessness. As a young warrior, he had found himself in some very compromising positions. But even backed into a corner, he could fight his way out. But as a toy? He was useless, powerless, and, to add insult to injury, duped by his own device.

Pitch's spell was wickedly ingenious. Not only was North unable to do anything other than what that devil commanded, but he was trapped as a toy with no real will of its own. He knew of no spell that could undo so many layers of entrapment. He couldn't even try to converse with Ombric and find a way out of this nightmare. He could only speak when Pitch told him to, and Ombric had not uttered a word since Pitch's spells were cast.

"You pathetic toys. Are you useless to me?" Pitch muttered in frustration.

"Yes, Master," replied North.

Pitch tossed them both into the snow with disgust. "The weapon is here—that much is certain. In time I'll find it. All the magic I may need is in those books of yours. I need no tutor."

A fresh snow had begun to fall. Cold flakes landed on North's face. *Not exactly a warrior's death,* North thought. *Or a wizard's.*

Then came a familiar flash of light—the light that Pitch despised above all others.

CHAPTER TWENTY-ONE

◦•◦

Laughter Is a Bitter Pill

THE HIGH HIMALAYAS WERE vast, all-encompassing, and silent. But all of that was shattered by the arrival of the spectral boy. The moments that followed were a burst of action and noise. A meteor-like explosion of pure light knocked Pitch away from North and Ombric.

As Pitch scrambled back up, he found the spectral boy standing before him, the diamond tip of his staff pointed inches away from Pitch's own chest plate at the key that activated the mechanical shell. Pitch recoiled instantaneously, the memory of having been in this situation before surging through him: a blind-

ing light, a dagger to his chest, centuries of imprisonment in that putrid cave. Well, not this time!

Pitch drew his sword and readied to finish the lad. But something caused him to stop short: the improbable sight of a cluster of reindeer galloping down from the low-lying clouds, thundering directly toward him. Riding the lead reindeer was a young girl waving a dagger with the furious skill of a seasoned swashbuckler. And—how could it be?—they were riding on a sort of mist of light!

Before Pitch could gather his senses, the girl and her company pounded to the ground. Snow flying in every direction, they stampeded around Pitch. Then the girl dove forward, clinging to the pummel of her saddle with one hand, scooping up North and Ombric with the other. Pitch glared in disbelief as the entire entourage leaped back onto the lighted mist and vanished into the sky. He swung back to the spectral boy. But the boy, too, was gone, only an echo of laughter that refracted from mountain to mountain remained. Like a splinter under the skin, it taunted and infuriated Pitch.

CHAPTER TWENTY-TWO
The Oddest Reunion

WHEN KATHERINE FELT THEY were far enough away from Pitch, she steered the reindeer toward what looked to be a safe and comfortable spot: a cave midway up one of the massive mountain peaks. Night was falling, but the spectral boy's glow was light enough for her to fully see the terrible predicament her two friends were in.

Somehow, that awful Pitch had turned North and Ombric into dolls—Ombric in a miniature wizard's hat, cloak, and staff; and North in his red and black coat, a sword the size of a pin in each tiny hand.

Their faces were blank, their stares unblinking.

"North? Ombric?" she whispered, choking back tears. "How can I save you?" Her worry was steadied by her determination. She would find a way to return them to themselves. She'd bring them back to Santoff Claussen. And she'd study every last book in Ombric's library—if it took her the rest of her life, she would learn a way.

The reindeer had nosed their way back to the edge of the cave, sensing Katherine's sorrow. They encircled her, the frosty haze of their breath warming the space. Outside, the wind began to pick up, spewing an otherworldly howl through the air. The spectral boy dimmed his staff and peered out carefully from the cave's entrance. Immediately he drew his head back in. The sky was dirty with countless Nightmare Men and Fearlings, and the boy knew they were searching for them. Dense clouds began to block every glimmer of moonlight. Night had brought out all of Pitch's tricks. The spectral boy could see that he and Katherine were hopelessly outnumbered.

He looked at Katherine as she sat on the cave floor rocking back and forth, holding her friends close to her. She'd wrapped the corners of her yellow coat around them. The boy had watched her often since that first night in the forest when she alone had been unafraid of the Fearlings. Then he'd seen her again up in the clouds. He'd never seen a Small One up *there* before. Her smile had enchanted him—made him feel happier than he could ever remember. Then, this very morning, he'd seen her friends—the old man and the young one with the red coat—in the clouds. But they left her behind! That didn't seem fair. So he'd been on his way to check on her when he'd heard her asking the owls to fetch the reindeer. She wanted to catch up to the Tall Friends. Well, who was better at playing catch than he! So he focused his powers on creating a highway of light and the girl knew just what to do.

But as they sped across the continent, the boy saw that she looked scared. She looked constantly at the compass hanging from her neck, then straight ahead. Only once did she take her eyes away from the horizon—to glance at him as he flew beside her. Why was she scared? He wasn't sure, but he knew she was not smiling. And he wanted to see that smile again.

Now they were trapped. How had he let her guide them to a cave, of all places? And he knew all about being trapped. Hadn't he been exactly that until his moonbeam came and set him free? Soon the Fearlings would find the cave, and then what?

The boy peeked past the cave's entrance once

more. The Fearlings were coming nearer. But the boy had an idea—a chase! The best chase ever!—and this time it would be more than just a game. He held the diamond tip of his staff close to his face and grinned at the moonbeam inside. He and the moonbeam had become comrades. The beam was ready. Then the boy looked back at Katherine one last time.

An instant later, he was gone. Holding his staff aloft and shining brighter than ever, the boy flew into the sky, swooping and circling till he was sure every one of Pitch's soldiers had spotted him. Then he rocketed toward the clouds. The armies of darkness banked left and followed.

The endgame was on!

CHAPTER TWENTY-THREE
The Longest Night

KATHERINE HEARD THE SPECTRAL boy laughing
as he led Pitch's legions away from her. How amazing
he was. Risking everything for her and her friends.

He was fast and clever, there was no doubt. Perhaps he could perform a new miracle that would save
them, or find help from some quarter that she did not
know.

But for now she must make sure they weren't discovered by any of Pitch's stragglers. She quickly and
quietly had the reindeer cover the entrance to the cave
by using their antlers to shovel snow from the floor

till there was only a small lookout hole left.

But despite the blockade, it was still terribly cold. Katherine's fingers ached; her toes were going numb. She had no means of building a fire, and even if she had, she knew even the thinnest tendril of smoke would let Pitch know where they were. So she wrapped North and Ombric more tightly in the collar of her coat and huddled against the reindeer, who were far more suited for the frigid weather.

As for North, though he could not move, couldn't even blink, his mind raced on. And what was this dashing bandit, this ex-Cossack, this long-feared warrior thinking? He was not plotting his battle plan or picturing how he would defeat Pitch. No. North was worrying about Katherine's coat. Was it warm enough? He imagined the coat he would make for her if they ever made it back to Big Root, using an old

Cossack trick of double-layering the fur. Katherine gave a shiver, and North's feelings of helplessness were excruciating—she *was* cold, colder and sadder than any child should be.

Katherine was also deeply tired. She struggled to stay alert, tried to focus on what to do next, but the rhythmic breathing of the reindeer soon lulled her into a gentle sleep, North and Ombric tucked tightly under her chin.

When children have nightmares, they struggle to awaken, knowing that comfort lies just beyond their tightly shut eyes. But for Katherine, the nightmare was all around her, and so sleep was her escape. She spent the night drifting in and out of dreams. But hers were no ordinary ones.

There's a rare kind of dream that children have, a dream that unfolds like a storybook, but a story in which the dreamer does not take part. They watch, instead, the adventures of someone dear to them in a sort of movie of the mind. And the dream Katherine was having starred Nicholas St. North. North was a hero of a thousand adventures. He was not a wizard, a thief, or a warrior, but a powerful figure of unending mirth, mystery, and magic, who lived in a city surrounded by snow.

This kind of dream is so rare that most dreamers do not understand the magic it holds; it plays in tandem somewhere else, the same exact adventure and images rolling through another person's sleep.

And that was what was happening now. As North lay there helplessly and nearly without hope, he began to see Katherine's dreams in his own head. A city of snow in a flurry of activity and him—as he'd never imagined himself or even thought possible—happy and at home. He was the master of this domain.

For the second time in as many weeks, North realized that this was how Katherine saw him. In the drawing she'd given him for the djinni's chest box, she'd depicted him grander than he was in real life. And now she saw him as having an important place in the world.

Then the dream did something that only dreams can do: It became a part of North, became *his* dream. It lived in his heart now and would never die.

With a violent suddenness the dream ended. North was awake again, but he could not see. Katherine's coat covered his eyes. There was a blast of cold air. Then shouts, and he felt himself being jerked up. He heard the furious neighing of the reindeer and the sound of hooves and antlers clattering against metal.

Pitch had found them.

North felt another jerk and heard Katherine screaming, "Get away!" Then something shadowy pressed tightly around him. Katherine's coat was gone from his face and he could see her curled in a tight ball on the ground, surrounded by Fearlings. The reindeer were struggling wildly in ropes and chains of shadows, but the restraints held tight, and they dashed their hooves on the cave floor with fury. North was caught in the grip of a Fearling. He was suddenly turned around and saw the giant face of his djinni glaring down at him, Pitch's laugh rumbled out from its metal chest.

"Little man," Pitch said in a voice oozing with malevolence, "how useless you've become." Then his gaze shifted to Katherine. "I once had a Fearling prince slip out of my grasp, but it won't happen again. But before I turn *you* into a Fearling princess, I want to hear one last scream." He smiled wickedly at the Fearling holding North. "Crush him. Now."

The Fearling threw North violently onto the rocky floor. The sound of his hitting had a sickening sharpness. The toy North lay shattered.

Katherine, using a might that surprised even herself, broke away from the Fearlings. She would *not* scream. She gathered the pieces of North's body quickly and carefully. Ombric had taught her—Ombric had taught them all—that magic's real power is belief. And she'd seen it happen with her own eyes. So it could happen again. It *had* to.

She raced to the back of the cave.

Pitch was just steps away. In a moment's time she'd be taken, turned into a Fearling. Pitch's cackle boomed through the cave. "What a feisty Fearling you'll be," he laughed. The djinni's robotic arms, the same ones that had carefully caught her that day back by Big Root, cut violently through the air. Then. They. Stopped. Pitch could not move closer. He strained with all the strength he possessed, but the machine arm would not obey. "This cannot be!" he hissed in disbelief.

Katherine didn't waste a second. Her hands worked nimbly, and as she set the last piece of North's form into place, she took a deep breath, and whispered Ombric's first spell, "I believe, I believe, I believe. Please be real again. This will work. I believe . . ."

But before Katherine could even finish her plea, a terrific rumbling came from outside the cave. At first she thought it was thunder, but as it grew closer, louder, she realized it was coming from the ground and the sky. She looked toward the cave entrance, as did Pitch and his Fearlings. The sky outside was brightening. The rumbling intensified until the cave began to shake. Outside could be heard the calls and howls of Fearlings and Nightmare Men.

Then, without any forewarning at all, the entire top of the mountain blasted away. They ducked down to shield themselves, but in the haze of snow and pulverized rock, they realized they were safe. They stood exposed now. In the open air they could now see all around. It was an epic sight. On every mountain and valley, on the ground and in the air above were swarms of Nightmare Men and Fearlings. Every inch was nasty with shadowy hordes. But closing in from all sides was a wave of magnificent hairy creatures, white as snow, as big as the bear, and armed to the teeth. They were cutting through Pitch's creatures like surf does to sand. With a deafening clap of thunder the clouds above parted and the moon shined down. From it came a fleet of moonbeams led by none other than the spectral boy. They raked the skies, felling every dark creature that faced them.

His anger sharpening to a deadly point, Pitch turned again to Katherine and the others. What he saw enraged him even more.

North stood before him. No longer a toy, but a man, with his head cocked back defiantly, his cape blowing in the wind, and a saber at the ready in each hand! Katherine, or something, had broken the spell!

"Dark and sinister imp," he said to Pitch with cheerful sarcasm, "how annoying you've become."

Then he fell on Pitch with a fury. Their blades struck at a pace that seemed impossible. Katherine could barely believe what she was seeing. North had returned and he would not be denied. If Pitch was faster than any human, then North was now his match. Their sabers exploded with strobes of fire and sparks. They taunted each other as they fought.

"How does it feel to have your own invention best you in every way?" challenged Pitch.

North smiled and replied, "What I make I can destroy."

"I've scuttled whole planets, burglar. You're just another inconvenience."

North shook his head, then lowered both his swords. He stood up straight, spread his arms, and closed his eyes. "Do your worst, Pitch," he said calmly.

"What sort of trick is this?" asked Pitch. "I can slice you in two before you can lift a sword." But there North stood, insultingly at ease. He even began to whistle.

Pitch could not resist. He swung his blade with all his might, but his metal arm stopped just an eighth of an inch from North's brow.

Pitch was flabbergasted yet again. North opened his eyes, glanced Katherine's way, and winked. "It's the drawing in his chest," he said slyly. "He can turn us into toys, but with his own hands he can't do us real harm. Your artwork is very powerful, my girl."

Pitch had just enough time to process what North said—and to realize he was beaten. For now.

Katherine almost giggled with relief and amazement.

Pitch looked out at the battle raging around him. He could see the tide going against his troops. He was no fool. He turned sharply back to North and Katherine. "I'll keep the djinni as a gift. Let's just say it 'suits' me." Then he took to the sky, transforming into the djinni's flying machine. Within seconds, he and his Fearlings were mere black specks on the horizon, vanishing westward, just ahead of the coming dawn.

CHAPTER TWENTY-FOUR

The Journey's End

ONLY MINUTES HAD PASSED since Pitch's retreat, but they had been filled with wonders and revelations.

Pitch's spell of enslavement had only partially afflicted Ombric. Like North's, his physical body had been turned into a toy, but eons ago, Ombric had learned how to separate his mind from his body. He called it "astral projection" and used it only rarely.

"It's quite risky," he explained to North. "One can never be entirely sure what the body may be up to while the mind is out and about, and it depletes one's energy rather severely. I'll be hungry for months now."

And, in fact, Ombric had been eating provisions from the infinity bag nonstop since he'd returned to his body. He seemed to relish telling North and Katherine about his adventure, for he paced back and forth excitedly.

The moment Pitch had cast his spell, he'd told them, Ombric had projected himself to the Temple of the Lunar Lamas. The Lunar Lamas were a mysterious brotherhood of holy men who devoted their lives to the study of the Moon. Their temple, or, as it was properly called, their Lunar Lamadary, had been Ombric's true destination throughout their journey.

History has no accurate record of how the Lunar Lamas had come into existence or how exactly they had become devoted to the Moon and the Man who ruled it. Ombric had first heard of them as a boy in Atlantis and even the greatest minds of that long-lost place found them allusive and confounding. But Ombric knew in his ancient bones that these men would at least be interested in Pitch's return and had to be helpful in ways no one else on Earth could be.

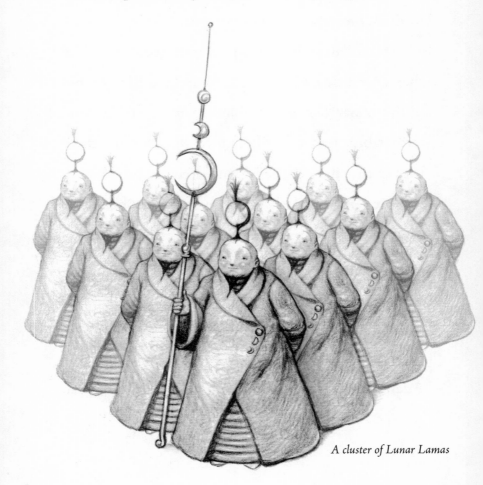

A cluster of Lunar Lamas

The Lunar Lamas were extremely secretive and cautious. They never made contact with the outside world, not even with wizards of Ombric's stature. And they had not been welcoming when Ombric first arrived. Ombric had pleaded with them: Did they have a relic from the *Moon Clipper*? Something that had fallen to Earth? Something of great power? But the Lamas had sworn to keep all they knew a secret until ordered otherwise.

Apparently, they had a way of conversing directly with the Man in the Moon, though it was invoked only under the most extraordinary circumstances.

"What circumstances could possibly be more extraordinary than these?!" Ombric had demanded. "Pitch is *here*! His hordes are on the other side of *these peaks*! The sworn enemy of your master has returned armed to the teeth and means to make something considerably more than mischief!!!!"

But the Lunar Lamas were the most serene men on Earth, and no amount of arguing could get them to hurry. They'd gathered in the courtyard, padding silently in silver slippers, their hands hidden in the sleeves of their billowing silk-spun robes, their round Moonlike faces as pleasant and inscrutable as melons.

"We appreciate your concern," said one Lama.

"We understand your frustration," said another.

"We sympathize completely," said the next.

"We regret the situation," said the fourth.

"We must receive a sign," said another.

"We hope you understand," said the last.

"Sorry," concluded the one who had spoken first, smiling.

Their response had left Ombric livid. It was fortunate that he was astrally projected, for had he been in physical form, he might have punched each and every holy man squarely in his Moon-shape face.

Then a most auspicious thing had occurred. Streaking down from the sky came the spectral boy. He landed in the courtyard of the Lamadary, skidding to a stop right in front of where Ombric and the Lamas stood, his staff in hand, the diamond dagger glowing brightly at its tip.

Ombric had recognized him immediately—it was the very same boy who'd driven away the Fearlings back in Santoff Claussen. And it had been instantly apparent that the Lamas had recognized him as well. Their response to the newcomer couldn't have surprised Ombric more. They'd murmured excitedly among themselves, then knelt and bowed until their foreheads touched the floor. Ombric drew a deep breath, willing himself to hold his tongue. And it took great, *great* restraint. Here he was, the greatest wizard in the land, and yet those Lamas were bowing—*bowing!*—to this . . . this . . . boy! Heads still pressed to the ground, the Lamas all began speaking at the same time.

"'Tis the sign we have been waiting for!"

"Since the beginning of our order!"

"The guardian of the Man in the Moon!"

"The one with the diamond dagger!"

"The one who stopped Pitch!"

"He is called Nightlight!"

Nightlight. Ombric had never seen that name in his ancient texts, the texts about the Golden Age. He eyed the boy. He seemed all arms and legs and grin, and he emitted the soft glow of a young firefly. Could this ghostly slip of a boy be of such importance?

The Lamas gestured toward a huge gong that

hung behind them, beckoning Ombric closer. It was clearly one of their most prized possessions. Ombric felt a shiver of great excitement as he examined it. The gong wasn't simply a beautiful instrument—the elaborate carvings were actually telling a story . . . the story of the Man in the Moon! "Tsar Lunar related it to us centuries ago," said the Grand High Lama. "It is as he saw, experienced, and remembered."

There it was, in picture after glorious picture as described by Tsar Lunar himself. The majestic *Moon Clipper* at full sail. The merry Moonbots and Moonmice. Ombric could barely still his mind to take it all in, and then, there, on the far side, was the part of the story that had always been a mystery to him. Ombric glanced from the boy in the picture to the boy in front of him. They were the same. It was true! This boy had been the loyal friend and

guardian of the young Man in the Moon. He had protected the Prince from nightmares, and his diamond dagger had pierced Pitch's black heart at the height of the great battle. It was this act that caused the great explosion that saved the Man in the Moon and sent Pitch's galleon plummeting to Earth, where it had crashed like a meteor and lay hidden deep under the ground for centuries. This spectral boy was a true hero.

"NIGHTLIGHT!" the Lamas shouted in unison.

"Nightlight, indeed," concurred Ombric with surprise.

The boy rocked on his heels before them, a puzzled look in his pale green eyes. It was so long ago, yet that name still existed within him as distant memory. He cocked his head, then shook it. What mattered to Nightlight was the *here and now*. The battle was still on! He swung his staff toward the sky. The Lamas and Ombric looked up. Pitch's minions were diving toward them. They'd followed Nightlight there, just as he'd hoped. He'd observed the Lunar Lamas, and he knew they had the best weapons against these shadowy creatures.

To Ombric's amazement, the Lamas switched from whispering statues to men of action. Bells rang. Horns blew. And a great rumbling, as if Earth itself were growling, filled the courtyard.

Ombric looked out through the columns that marked the entrance of the building. A legion of giant, hairy snow creatures was gathering outside of the Lamadary, already in military formation. It was an army of Abominable Snowmen! Ombric had read about them but had never seen one. They had an amazing arsenal of gleaming clubs, swords, and

Yeti & Their Weaponry

Some Yeti stand.

Yeti arrow gun with mountain-to-mountain accuracy

Quiver

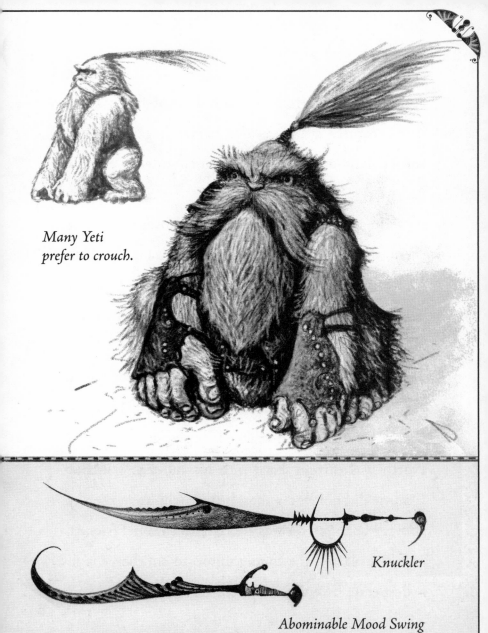

Many Yeti
prefer to crouch.

Knuckler

Abominable Mood Swing

Dinner Knife

spearguns, all forged with the dust of fallen stars. The creatures stilled as the Lamas began to blow their tribal horns, the horns that sounded the battle charge.

And charge they did, with Nightlight leading them, through the mountains and toward the peak where Pitch had trapped Katherine and the others. The Lamas accompanied the army, whirling like tornadoes, dervishes, banshees!

Ombric instantly projected himself after them. And arrived, evidently, at the most opportune time—just as the battle had reached its tipping point and North was turning back into his full-size self. But Ombric did not know that; he was still up in the sky above. He feared he was too late to save his friends, and had blasted the mountaintop to smithereens in a desperate attempt to intervene. Though Ombric hated to admit it, he now felt he'd overreacted, ever so slightly.

"Most unsubtle bit of conjuring," he conceded as he finished his story. "More like something you, Nicholas, would have done in your early days. . . . I could have accidentally hurt someone—one of the reindeer or even young Katherine. Can't imagine what got into me." Even an astral projection can blush with embarrassment, and Ombric, for the first time in several hundred years, did that exact thing. North laughed in astonishment.

"You're as red as the setting sun, old man!" North teased.

"He was just worried about us," Katherine interrupted.

"Harumph," Ombric muttered, then kept himself busy searching among the pulverized bits of the mountaintop until he found his discarded toy body and projected himself back into it. Within a few moments he had broken the last vestige of Pitch's spell and returned, as North had, to his flesh-and-blood self.

North narrowed his eyes. "How did you do that? And furthermore, how did I do that?"

The wizard paused and regarded his apprentice. "You know, a daydream properly utilized can be the most powerful force in the universe. One need only dream of freedom to begin to break the spell of enslavement."

North nodded. His teacher was right. But he knew that for him it was something else. "It was more than a daydream that brought me back, old man." He looked down at Katherine. "You saved me, in many ways . . ." He reached for his compass that hung from

Katherine's lapel. His gift had served them both rather well. Katherine had her great adventure and North had found a friend for life. He turned to the old wizard. "I came to your village in search of treasure. But I found a better one than I ever supposed."

Ombric looked at the ground and was quiet for a moment. When he spoke it was with real and gentle compassion. "I told you once there was no magic in the world that can change a human heart. You've proven me wrong, my young friend." Then he smiled fully for the first time in centuries.

But the friends couldn't dwell on this lovely moment. Now that everyone was safe, they were rushed to the Lunar Lamadary. The Lamas had judged them worthy to receive the highest honor their brotherhood could bestow, and the ceremony was ready to begin.

✦ ✦ ✦

"There is no place on Earth where the light is as bright and clear as in the Himalayan Mountains," Ombric said cheerfully as he, North, and Katherine stood atop the tower of the Lunar Lamadary. "No other place is as close to the Moon. Why, we're on the highest spot in the world!" And one of the most beautiful. The Lamadary was a simple palace of lapis lazuli and opal mosaics, and it managed to keep the cool, serene feeling of moonlight, even in the morning sun.

Bells and gongs began to ring from all around the temple that sat in the center of the Lamadary. Katherine couldn't stop staring at its roofline, where thousands of silver bells chimed with the slightest wisp of wind.

"What do you suppose we'll be given?" she asked.

"I hope it's food," North joked. "Ombric has

already eaten everything in sight, and I'm afraid he'll start chewing on my coat."

Ombric shushed them both as they entered the courtyard. The entire brotherhood of Lamas stood at attention, as did an honor guard of the giant shaggy warriors.

"What are they called again?" whispered Katherine.

"Those in the outside world call them Abominable Snowmen, but the Lamas refer to them as Yetis," Ombric whispered back.

The great hulking creatures had never seen a child before and were fascinated by Katherine. As were all the denizens of the Lamadary, especially the half dozen birds, enormous in size, their wings silver-tipped, which the Lamas cared for. They were the Great Snow Geese of the Himalayas, a species of bird unknown to any outside the Lamadary. Ombric mused, "I must remember to notate these geese in my notebooks."

Katherine had already included them in her journal. She was the only child in the history of the world who had ever seen them! "I should very much like to ride one. They are big enough," she whispered loudly, but Ombric held a finger to his lips, and she knew it was truly time to be quiet.

The trio was ushered to the center of the courtyard. The reindeer grazed along the edges, raising their antlers in salute as they walked by. Katherine could barely take her eyes off the beautiful gong Ombric had told them about. She scanned the carvings for her friend, the spectral boy—Nightlight. (She was glad to finally know he had a name.) *Where is Nightlight?* she wondered. *Of all people, he should be here.* But the ceremony began without him.

The Grand High Lama, who looked exactly like all the other Lamas except for the gilded scepter he carried, stepped forward and struck the great gong. It made the most melodious sound that the visitors had ever heard.

As it rang out, the gong began to turn from solid metal to a clear, glasslike substance. Through its milky translucence, they could see the Moon. Murmurs and speculation filled the air. Could it be? Was this really the moment the Lamas—*everyone*—had been waiting for? As the gong's reverberations quieted, the Moon seemed to swell in size. Then a face emerged from the craters. Immediately the Lamas knelt down in reverence. Here before them was the kindest, gentlest face imaginable.

"Tsar Lunar!" gasped Ombric. He caught Katherine's elbow.

Yes. It was the Man in the Moon.

His image flickered and waned, like light through lush, swaying trees. His image was not stable, but dotted with shadows and static. Still, there was no denying that he was there. His voice was calm and velvety—almost musical.

"Greetings, my valiant friends," he began. "You have faced the greatest evil of any age, and yet you never wavered. Each of you was willing to sacrifice everything for this cause. Such bravery. Such skill. Such wisdom you each have shown! For that you have my deepest thanks."

North, Ombric, and Katherine, feeling humbled and self-conscious, gave awkward bows.

"But this fight is far from over," the Man in the Moon continued. "Pitch lives and will not stop. Can you—will you—continue the fight?"

An audience with Tsar Lunar,
the Man in the Moon!

The three looked at one another for a quick moment, but they knew what their answer would be. North unsheathed his sword and held it at attention. Ombric did the same with his staff, and Katherine raised her dagger.

The Man in the Moon smiled down at them. It was a smile of such warmth and friendliness that it made any who saw it feel as though no matter what trials were to come, all would be well.

"Then you will need help," said Tsar Lunar.

At this, the Grand Lama pulled from his robe an ancient weapon, and held it out to them. It was a sword so unusual that North, who thought he'd known (and used) every weapon in creation, stepped forward to take a closer look. On its blade was a golden orb that glowed, and on its tip was a crescent moon.

"There are four other pieces of my *Moon Clip-*

per that fell to Earth in the last Battle of the Golden Age," the Man in the Moon told them. "If these five pieces are brought together, they will become a most formidable weapon against Pitch. This first piece was my father's sword. But this is not merely a sword for battle. Within its workings are many of the secrets of the Golden Age. Whoever wields it will need great learning, wisdom, and courage. Who among you shall take it?"

Instantly both North and Katherine thought of Ombric, but before they could speak, the wizard stepped forward. He took the sword from the Grand Lama and examined it with his usual intensity. *Oh, the wonders this sword must contain,* he thought. The ancient secrets it will finally reveal. But then he raised one eyebrow and gazed at North, and in one quick move handed him the weapon.

"You are my apprentice no more," he said with a warmth North had only heard him ever use when addressing Katherine. "You have learned all the lessons I can teach and have more than earned this."

North was stunned. And for the first time in his life, truly unsure. "Ombic . . . I'm not ready or deserving. You waited all your life—"

"Ombric's right," interrupted Katherine quietly. North looked at her, searched her young, brave face. She had always known what was best for him. *In her own way she may even be wiser than Ombric,* he thought.

So North took the sword. As he held it in his hand, he felt not a great rush of emotions, but a strange calm. A certainty of purpose. A sense of belonging that he had never known before. As if his whole life lay before him and he knew how it would play out. It would be like Katherine's dream.

He looked up at the Man in the Moon's image. The Man in the Moon was waiting for his answer.

"You have my pledge to use it wisely and well," said North. "Now, and always."

Watching from the highest tower of the Lamadary was Nightlight, unseen by anyone. His focus was distracted; he was scanning the nearby mountains for any sign of Pitch. But he wanted to join his friends. He held his staff close to his face. The little moonbeam in the diamond dagger tip—this moonbeam who had started this whole great drama into motion on a winter's night that now seemed so long ago—could sense his longing. It glowed brightly and seemed to say, "Go on. We're safe now." Nightlight laughed his perfect laugh and flew down to join them.

He landed in the Lamadary, quick and playful,

and, taking Katherine's hand, pulled her into the sky. The Lamas cheered. The Snow Geese honked. Ombric grabbed a huge cookie that he'd had hidden in his robe and cheerfully devoured it. Nightlight and Katherine spiraled around in the air. The Man in the Moon glowed brighter than the Lamas had ever seen. And for that one day, all their worlds seemed safe and right.

The weeks that followed were quiet. They'd all earned a good rest. Ombric ate so much that the Yetis (who, oddly, were accomplished chefs) could barely keep up with his appetite.

"I doubt we'll ever have another stretch of days as calm as these again," mused North to Katherine as they stood on the temple's parapet days later. Katherine was sketching the Snow Geese into her journal. "I suspect these are our halcyon days," North added.

"Halcyon days?" she asked.

"Ah, one of those ancient words Ombric is so fond of using. It means happy and carefree." North grinned and added, "I prefer battles and adventures."

Katherine knew what he meant. All these new amazements were in their lives. Abominable Snowmen. Giant Snow Geese. Lunar Lamas. She wondered if Santoff Claussen would still feel like home. She closed her eyes for a moment to remember her life as it had been. Images of the villagers—Old William, little Fog, the bear, Petrov—and Big Root, all of it, flooded her memory. And she missed them, but she'd also become accustomed to all this danger and adventuring. Still, despite all this, she felt an odd sort of peace.

"It's the bliss of victory," North explained to her. "It's a feeling you'll have to get used to."

Katherine's face grew serious. "But we didn't defeat Pitch."

"True, but we lived to fight another day."

Katherine thought about that. Then she tugged a fresh stick of charcoal from her coat pocket and began to draw. North looked out toward the horizon and thought of the dream Katherine had given him. The gleaming city that he would someday build and the man he might become.

A strange and exciting future lay ahead for both of them. The possibilities were endless. Battles would be fought. Wonders revealed. Many journeys. Many lands. Many joys. Many sorrows.

But stories all . . .

THE NEXT CHAPTER
IN OUR ONGOING SAGA WILL BE

◆

E. ASTER
BUNNYMUND
AND THE BATTLE OF
THE WARRIOR EGGS